I0524440

KAI

N GRAY

BOOKS

KAI

N. GRAY

VIRGIL
BOOKS

By N Gray

Shifter Days, Vampire Nights & Demons in Between

Twisted

Lady Hawk and Her Mountain Man

Hidden Shifter

Wolf

Wolf Retreat

Night Hunter

The Fixer

Kai

Lee

Flynn

Jude

Scout Thorne

The Secret Tomb

Murder of Crows

Blaire Thorne

Ulysses Exposed

Voodoo Priest

Butterflies and Hurricanes

Salvation

Underworld Legacy

The Dana Mulder Suspense Thriller Series

Deadly Pattern

Devil Mountain

Chasing Evil

Nightcrawler

Horror

What's for Dinner

Creature Features

Monster Features

Thrillers

Lady Killer

More from N Gray

writing as Natalie Michaels

Steve Campbell Psychological Suspense Thrillers

The Last Girl

The Bone Forest

The White Dahlia

I See You

Death in the City

More from N Gray

writing as SD Syns

The Diaries

Red Lace Diaries

www.ngraybooks.com

Vinci Books

vinci-books.com

Published by Vinci Books Ltd in 2026

1

Copyright © N Gray 2022

The author has asserted their moral right to be identified as the author of this work in accordance with the Copyright, Designs and Patents Act 1988. This work is a work of fiction. Names, characters, places and incidents are the product of the author's imagination or are used fictitiously. Any resemblance to actual persons, living or dead, places and incidents is entirely coincidental.

All rights reserved. No part of this publication may be copied, reproduced, distributed, stored in any retrieval system, or transmitted in any form or by any means, including photocopying, recording, or other electronic or mechanical methods, nor used as a source for any form of machine learning including AI datasets, without the prior written permission of the publisher.

The publisher and the author have made every effort to obtain permissions for any third party material used in this book and to comply with copyright law. Any queries in this respect should be brought to the attention of the publisher and any omissions will be corrected in future editions.

A CIP catalogue record for this book is available from the British Library.

Paperback ISBN: 9781036702243

The EU GPSR authorised representative is Logos Europe, 9 rue Nicolas Poussion, 17000 La Rochelle, France contact@logoseurope.eu

Chapter One

KAI

I entered the hallway and into the cavernous room. I assessed whether any of the doors had been breached or if any artifacts Léon stored in his renovated warehouse had been stolen or damaged.

Everything was as it should be and stepped into the kitchen I shared with three other shifters. I switched on the kettle and added a tea bag into my favorite mug. A smell caught my attention, and followed the stench to the basin; inside sat dirty dishes and leftover food with flies buzzing around. When I opened the dishwasher, it was full, too.

While the kettle boiled, I burst through Jude's door and the were-tiger jackknifed out of bed, his fists out readying to fight.

Jude narrowed his eyes, realizing there was no threat, giving me the middle finger. "Asshole," Jude said, raising his hands above his head to shield his eyes from the blinding lights. "I was sleeping."

"It's your turn to empty the dishwasher."

Jude groaned and fell back into bed. "You're worse than my freakin' mother. Give me ten more minutes."

"Now, Jude, the kitchen stinks. Do you want cockroaches again or worse, the stench of rotten food hovering throughout the warehouse?"

"Christ! All right, all right, I'm up," Jude moaned, kicking off the covers, and climbed out of bed. He pushed against my chest as he stomped past. He headed in the kitchen's direction, scratching his ass as he made a show of how upset he was that I disturbed his sleep.

Jude reluctantly opened the dishwasher tray and unpacked the dishes into their rightful spots while I finished making tea.

"Morning." Lee strode in, flicked my ear and darted to the other side of the kitchen, narrowly missing my backhand.

"One day I'm going to get you where it hurts."

"I can't wait. Maybe then you'll get that old man stick out your ass," Lee said, drinking water from the open faucet, then closed it.

"Someone needs to keep you in line or this place would be in chaos and Léon would bleed you dry."

Lee grunted.

"Morning." Flynn entered and roared. He removed a mug from the cupboard and started making coffee. "You should rather drink this, Kai," — he tapped the coffee pot. "It gives you great hair." He combed his fingers through his jet-black hair.

Lee laughed. "Man, I still find it strange your mane goes sun-soaked yellow when you change."

"Yet, it stays gloriously dark around the edges." Flynn wiggled his eyebrows. "The darker the mane the more powerful the lion," he roared again.

2

"We get it," Jude mumbled. "It's not necessary to rip out the measuring tapes every morning, we all know you're the *bigger* animal."

"We're quicker though." Lee elbowed me.

I nodded. "That may be true, Flynn, but I prefer tea," I said, placing my cup on the table. "You two still okay for tonight?"

"Yes," Flynn and Jude said simultaneously.

"I'd do anything for you to get laid and to get off my back about the dishwasher," Jude mumbled into the dishwasher and closed it. "I on the other hand am always happy." He arched an eyebrow, no doubt reminding us he always had a lady keeping him company. "'Cause at night the monster ladies love to come out and play."

"Yeah, and they steal from the Master," I said dryly.

Jude harrumphed. "It happened once, Kai. Are you ever going to drop it?"

"Maybe when you start doing your chores without us having to ask you."

"Why can't we get someone to clean around here."

No-one answered Jude because we had this conversation with him numerous times before. Léon had already advised against anyone or a cleaning company to clean the warehouse because of the nature of the items he stored here.

Cleaning up after ourselves was part of our job. And besides, no-one would want to clean up after a bunch of animals, anyway; I grinned at the thought, leaning into the chairback.

I listened to the other men's banter and quietly sipped my tea. Jude was into any woman who would have him, while Flynn was a picky. Lee and I had been so busy lately we hadn't had time to find women. Hopefully tonight we'd break our dry spell.

As the others joked around a part of me wished I had found my mate. I wasn't an alpha male who led the pack, but a beta male who ranked high within the were-leopard leap, along with my best friend Lee. Beta males did what was necessary to keep the pack strong and followed through on alpha orders. And it was beta males who usually only found their mates later in life or worse yet, never at all. And since I was not a natural born were-leopard, my chances were slim.

Every time I heard about beta shifters finding their mate, it left a sour taste in my mouth. Although I didn't have many one-night stands, I was getting tired of them. In today's world of quickies and hook-up culture, I still hoped my *one* was out there waiting for me.

I wanted someone to bond with, to share my life with and to cherish forever. The thought of waking up next to the same girl every single morning made my heart swell.

I wanted to know everything there was to know about that one woman. I wanted to commit every line on her body to memory. To know what made her scream my name as we made love. Sharing our thoughts for the future, and maybe even kids.

I wanted all of that and more. Unfortunately, I would have none of that.

I learned not to expect anything on my night out with Lee, and tonight would be no different. Lee might find a girl interested enough in him and bed her, or he'd just do it at the club. While I usually stood by the bar and drank.

Going out was more for Lee's benefit than for myself. And even though Lee knew this, it didn't stop him from dragging me along.

A hollow uneasiness settled within my chest but I made

peace with it. This was my life now. I would forever be alone, a dedicated worker to the Master Vampire of Sterling Meadow, and committed to Sebastian who led the leopards.

I stepped out of the shower as Lee waltzed in the communal bathroom with only his towel slung over his shoulder.

"I hope you're ready for all the ladies we're about to meet?" Lee said with a mischievous smirk. "And you got enough rest."

"You're bad for my reputation," I said, keeping up with the bravado. When I reached the door, I added. "It's not like we haven't been out before."

"I know we've been out. It's just we've only been to Léon's clubs and I'm tired of fangers. Have you decided where we're going first?"

"I thought you had a place in mind."

"No," he said, furrowing his brows.

"Okay, let me ask Jude then, he knows them all."

Once dressed, I found Jude eating in one of the private rooms. He sat in a chair made of gold with engravings etched into it.

I whistled. "Léon is going to murder you when he sees

these recordings." My eyes flitted to the cameras in each corner.

Jude always ate in this room; he said he felt like a king. He rested his feet on the golden coffee table while he ate chow mein out of the box.

"You know he never checks. Besides, you do such a stellar job here that nothing goes wrong. And he trusts you." He shoveled a mouthful of noodles. "Unless you plan on telling him?" he added as he chewed with bits of sauce spilling down his chin.

"Not yet, but if you continue using it as a dining room, I will. Anyway, that's not why I'm looking for you. Which club would you say is the best one? We've kinda lost touch with what's out there and one that doesn't belong to Léon—"

"There are a few, but my favorite is owned by the Russians. But don't go there though. They don't like our *kind*." He arched an eyebrow.

"I knew the Russians were in town, but I didn't know they already owned a nightclub."

"They were quick, but oh my gods, it's the best one. Again," — he pointed his chopsticks at me, — "do not go. Those guys are crazy and will kill you. They only allow humans in."

"How do you get in?"

"I enter with my human friends. It's the only way. They have a bear bouncer to sniff out the riff-raff. Just don't let him catch your leopard stink. Maybe blend in with some women and their perfume. He's one of a handful of shifters allowed on the property, and he is one vicious animal. I saw him rip apart a were-rat in the alley. It was nasty stuff, man." Jude shuddered and shoved the chopsticks into the box. "Thanks, you just killed my appetite."

"Give me the addresses for the other clubs and include that one. We might drive by."

"Sure, but don't do it, man. If you don't know how to blend in, it's not worth it." He stared at my clothing. "You might get in." One side of his mouth curled upward.

Chapter Three

KAI

I entered *Spiders* nightclub first, with Lee trailing behind me. There was no dress code or entrance fee. Which usually meant one thing—the riff-raff frequented here.

The place smelled of cheap cigars, alcohol and vomit. In a corner stood two men wearing leather; their ears had large flesh tunnels in their earlobes adorned with black earrings. They had snouts instead of noses as they had partially shifted into their hog beast.

A woman danced on stage, or rather slithered. Her tail rattled as she danced. When she reached the center of the stage, she gripped the pole with four arms and pulled herself up, an arm let go of the pole, removing her top. The hard rattles at the end of her tail shook and vibrated hypnotically. Her skin as smooth as porcelain and her raven hair cascaded passed her shoulders. Her breasts natural and firm.

Lee gawked at the snake-lady. I nudged him and he wiped his mouth dry.

"Oh my gods, she's beautiful."

"And deadly horned. Look at her head."

Lee raked his eyes up her body, her breasts, then widening them when he saw the two horns on either side of her head.

"She's deceptively poisonous. I would advise against meeting that one."

Lee shuddered as he forced himself to look away. "I need a stiff drink." He corrected the bulge in his pants and turned toward the bar.

I chuckled knowing Lee was easy to please when it came to women—they all did it for him. I on the other hand had a type and reptiles weren't it. I knocked twice on the wooden counter to get the barmen's attention.

"What's your poison?" the bartender said when he reached us.

"Two double shots of Tequila." I left money on the bar while the bartender poured our drinks.

I elbowed Lee, pushing his shot closer to him. "To all the pussy cats you gonna meet," I said, winking wickedly and downed my drink.

Lee downed his drink, scrunched his face at the awful taste and slammed his glass on the counter, alerting the barmen for a refill.

"I hate those things, but it gives me such a buzz. It's just unfortunate we have to drink a shit-ton before it does anything," he said, grinning.

The bartender refilled our glasses, Lee paid for this round.

We downed the shots, slammed our glasses on the counter simultaneously and turned around, scanning the dance floor. Men sat along the walls, with only a handful of women in-between. A couple stood near them, one in the corner, and then there was the magnificent snake-lady on stage.

"I must be honest. This place doesn't have enough women," I said with disappointment.

"Yeah, let's go to the next place."

The next nightclub had a queue all the way around the block. Lee grumbled when he saw it went right around the second block as well.

"There's no way we're getting in there tonight. Right, what's the next one."

The next establishment was the same as the first one; except it had more drunk men than women. We exited with a half an empty bottle of Tequila.

"Now what?" Lee asked, finishing the liquid and throwing it in the trashcan. "I don't discriminate, but I prefer the delicate touch of a woman. That place," — he thumbed behind him, — "was just too much testosterone for me."

I glanced at the list in my hand. There was only one place left. "We could try this one." I pointed at the word.

"*Stingray*," Lee sighed. "I've heard about it. They might not welcome us."

"We can go to one of Léon's clubs or back home—"

"No way. We're always going to his clubs. I love them, they have desirable women but they're mostly vampires. And I don't want to go back to the warehouse. It's still early. Let's check out *Stingray*," — he shrugged, — "maybe it's not so full."

I drove slowly past *Stingray* nightclub; blue, yellow, and green lights alternated as they struck the glass with their colorful strobes. I felt the music vibrations all the way to our car. Smoke emitted out the entrance as the bouncer spoke to a group of ladies.

I found the closest parking spot and killed the engine. Glancing over my shoulder at the warehouse, I had a sense of uneasiness spreading through my body. The tall dark bouncer flexed his impressive muscles as he pushed a man to the curb, pointed at something in the distance as he yelled at him never to return. The man crawled to his car and drove away.

"Maybe we shouldn't." I squeezed the door handle but kept it closed.

"It will be fine. We're cats, we run faster." Lee climbed out and slammed the door.

I hated when Lee did that; he assumed just because we're shifters, we could run away from anything. We could do a lot more than humans, but we weren't immortal; we'd die someday. It was just a matter of how much trouble we'd be in when that day arrived.

I ran my fingers through my short brown hair and exhaled sharply. I scratched the stubble on my chin and doubted I was in the best condition to catch any woman's attention.

We'd been working non-stop the last few years with hardly any time to play. With Sebastian and Greg becoming the alpha leaders of the leap, I knew we would be needed there and at the warehouse. Flynn and Jude were excellent shifters, and we got on, but... they were sloppy. And we desperately needed a break.

Finally, I gave into temptation and climbed out, locking the car.

It was risky entering a human only nightclub. As much as I wanted an evening away from leap and vampire business, being recognized as a shifter inside this club could result in our untimely death. This was a Russian nightclub after all, and they didn't take lawbreaking lightly. Lee and I had been best friend since the start and helped each other when trouble found us, and tonight wouldn't be different.

The mountain of a bouncer glowered over the line of patrons waiting to enter *Stingray*. We stood behind a group of rowdy men when two women came into the line behind us, smiling sweetly.

Lee elbowed me, wiggling his eyebrows. He turned around and started speaking to them.

The line moved up. The bouncer came in my line of sight. The four men in front of me laughed and joked. Two of them whistled at ladies who walked past to join the line behind the other girls. They blurted obscenities at the ladies, who blushed in response and avoided eye contact with the group of men.

The bouncer pointed at me. I glanced over my shoulder. When I turned back to face the bouncer, he approached.

I grabbed Lee's forearm. Lee stopped talking. The bouncer reached for us, but instead of taking hold of me, the bouncer grabbed the man in front.

"If you can't behave here, there's no way you'll behave in here." The bouncer pointed at a sign on the wall that read, *'While you wait, please do so respectfully'*.

"Hey man, everybody chill. We're cool," the man said as he placed a calm hand on the bouncer's shoulder. "We're all friends here."

"Don't touch me," the bouncer growled, pulling the man out of the line and shoved him away. "Get away before I pummel your faces into the concrete."

The man who had spoken raised his hands and nodded.

"Yeah, sure. We're going. No harm, no foul." He pulled on his friend's shirt. "Let's bounce."

The men crossed the road and climbed into a Maserati Levante. They were far too young to afford something like that. They barely had facial hair.

The bouncer returned to the front and allowed a group of women to enter.

Lee continued flirting with the two women behind us, but instead of joining their conversation, I stared at the men sitting in the Maserati. They didn't leave. They glowered at the club as they spoke. No doubt conspiring to do something.

When we finally reached the front, the bouncer gave us the stink eye. Then his eyes flitted to the two women hanging onto us, he allowed us access.

I was grateful Lee could be charming when he wanted to. With the girls help, we were able to access the venue. It wasn't as if we were trying for territory by pissing against the wall to lay claim to the building. We came for a good time.

As I stepped through the door, the heat smacked me in the face and the music was loud. Sweat beaded on my forehead and dripped down my back.

I followed Lee and the two women to the bar and ordered another round of Tequila shots.

The redhead, Kimberly something, clung to me while laughing at Lee's silly jokes.

I should be enjoying myself, but I wasn't. There was something indescribable about tonight I couldn't put a finger on. It wasn't the redhead pawing me like she'd never held a man before, but something else. I could almost taste it in the change of atmosphere.

I glanced around the club and that hollow feeling inside

intensified. Perhaps it was the part missing a mate, or I was having an off night. But the more I thought about it, the hollower I felt. And stranger thoughts swirled inside my head.

In all the years I'd been a shifter, I always felt as though a part of myself was missing. Whether it was parts of my soul, or the human part I'd lost, but the feeling sharpened tonight. There was something here that stirred within my chest, to the point that it ached.

I glanced at Lee who carried on like he always did—full of jokes and smiles—nothing disturbed him.

"Let's dance," the redhead said, pulling on my hand.

I groaned inwardly, not feeling like dancing, but didn't want to be rude either. She was pleasant looking with big brown eyes and long red hair. I followed her onto the dance floor anyway, with Lee and her friend beside them.

The music drowned out my thoughts as we danced. My body moved, but I didn't feel the music like I should. It felt superficial and forced. And I felt removed from my body not understanding why.

Lee gyrated against the woman beside him.

When I heard the redhead's name was Tiffany, I didn't care. I wasn't interested in her or her friend and would soon forget their names.

I danced, trying to feel the rhythm of the music in my soul, but it wasn't there. Casting an eye around the room of moving fevered bodies. The sweaty humans laughed, drank and danced. A woman had fallen to the ground without spilling her drink. Her partner helped her back onto her feet and they careened toward an empty chair. The smell of sweat, alcohol and arousal filled the large building.

One thing I realized surveying the humans, they were slow, docile creatures; weak and stubborn. When someone bumped into me, slurring an apology, I didn't push back. My shoulder sagged as I thought about leaving the dance area to blend with the shadows.

I reached for Lee to tell him I was sitting down when my eyes locked on her legs; toned and curvy. My heart skipped a beat as my eyes swept over her from heels to head; she wore a knee-high skirt that hugged her hips and ass, causing my body to twitch. She wore a low-cut white blouse with a black lace bra peeking through the see-through material.

I swallowed hard, but my throat remained dry.

She glanced from one side of the nightclub to the other, searching. Her neat raven hair shoulder length, framing her cerulean-colored eyes and delicate features.

Lee grabbed my shoulder, bringing me out of a trance.

"Hey, man, what are you gawking at?" Lee asked, glancing over his shoulder. "Oh my gods, no wonder you're drooling. I'd fuck her right on the dance floor."

"Hey!" I slammed my fist into his chest. I felt protective over her and didn't understand why.

"Ow man, it's just a saying. Christ. She's definitely a ten. Go speak to her while I keep these two company. Or, I can go to her and you take these two?" Lee said with a sly smile.

Not needing encouragement, I pushed Lee aside, turned, and slowly headed in her direction.

I didn't know who she was, but I had to speak to her, ask her name and introduce myself. One thing was clear, I had to know more about her.

My leopard pushed to the front; he liked what he saw, too.

She drew me to her in a way I never experienced before; as if hypnotized and led straight to my death—if it meant spending the last minutes of my life with her, I'd die a happy shifter.

My breathing labored and my chest ached. I wiped damp hands on my jeans, heart racing as I closed the gap. My legs shook with each step as I fought for control over my body; my leopard wanted out, and wanted her.

I dragged a steady breath over my teeth as my leopard smashed to the surface, yearning for release. My beast wanted her; he wanted to claim her. Now.

I reminded myself this was a *human only* nightclub. Nobody could know who or what I was. The risk of exposure wasn't worth it and fought for control.

The raven beauty's eyes danced over the people and stopped when she spotted my approach. Her long dark lashes framed her blue eyes, below them the delicate slope of her nose and full lips sending my heart fluttering when I envisioned them on my body.

When our eyes locked—our world slowed. Time stood still as I reached for her, closing the distance. The loud music drowned out by her beauty. We were the only two people in that moment.

I dared not avert my eyes for fear she would disappear, and it was only a figment of my desperate imagination. For I knew in this moment, it was real, and true.

Swallowing the dry lump in my throat. The corners of my mouth curved upward and reached my eyes.

My gaze lingered on her breasts but I quickly glanced at her face, maintaining my smile.

She arched an eyebrow, not impressed.

"Hi," I said smoothly, holding out my hand.

Her eyes flitted from my hand to my face, hesitating. "Hi," she finally said, reaching for my outstretched hand.

The moment we touched, electricity passed through us that set my blood on fire. I warmed from within as my beast rippled beneath the surface. A low growl escaped my lips, and I hoped she didn't hear.

She kept her hand in mine, leaned closer and said, "My name is Naomi."

"Kai." I lifted her hand to my mouth and gently kissed it.

The sound of her giggle sent a pleasurable ripple through my body, causing my smile to broaden—I enjoyed that sound.

"I didn't know men still did that," Naomi said, her blue eyes filled with curiosity, her hand unmoving.

"Only the good ones," I winked wickedly.

"I've never seen you here before." Naomi's cheeks reddened. She glanced away, trying to hide the fact that her body had betrayed her.

"It's my first time here, but I'm glad I came." I moved close enough to smell her sweet scent. When she didn't step away from me, I took another step closer and said near the shell of her ear. "I do, however, regret not coming sooner." I moved in her line of sight and smiled sincerely.

"Naomi!" She flinched when someone yelled her name. A man dressed in a black suit, with shaved hair and dark beady eyes approached from a room at the back of the nightclub. "Sacha wants you now." His tone was deep and throaty; it held an edge of a warning that if she didn't do as she was told, there would be consequences.

I didn't appreciate how she was being spoken to by someone she worked with and stood taller. I'd gladly fight this bouncer, but didn't know the circumstances of Naomi's employment and didn't want to ruin it for her.

As I thought that, I knew I wanted to provide for her, too. I wasn't a wealthy man, but I would do everything in my power to give her what she wanted.

My mouth dropped open by the revelation and confusion of it all. It was not like me to think this way over a woman and certainly not at first glance. These thoughts were ridiculous, but not. I would protect her, and would provide for her. My instincts to be everything for her took over my rational side of thinking. And my beast liked it. Beast wanted her.

"I have to go." She glanced at the man who'd called her, then back at me.

I didn't know this stunning woman standing in front of me, but I felt her hesitation; either she didn't want to leave or she didn't want to go to Sacha.

When she caught me staring longingly at her, she whispered. "Don't leave. I'll find you."

Her cheeks still held a pink glow, and I couldn't help but think it was because of me. We shared something in our brief encounter, and I knew she felt it too.

It was something I had only heard of from other shifters; those born of their beast would find their true mate with ease. When they had explained to me how it made them feel, how they were the only two people in that room and felt it with every inch of their body, and every part of their soul. That's how I felt with her.

I watched Naomi saunter toward the back door and glanced over her shoulder at me before disappearing. A way of telling me she meant what she'd said, even though we'd only just met.

I committed her face and body to memory, and would give anything to be her skirt; cupping her ass and hugging her body.

I felt a need stir within, an awakening like no other.

When a hand grabbed my shoulder, I twisted the hand away from me until it snapped.

"Jesus, Kai, fuck man. That's my hand you just broke."

"You should know better than to sneak up on me."

Lee snapped the joint back into place and massaged his wrist. He elbowed me. "Look man, those assholes are back."

I kept my attention on the door Naomi had used and needed to remain in an area where she could easily find me. If I wasn't near that door, I may never see her again.

Lee pulled on my shoulders, forcing me to look. When I turned in the other direction, I saw the four men from the line. Somehow, they'd gained entry. The bouncer would have remembered them, yet they strolled inside and to the bar like they owned the place.

I recognized their attitudes and it meant one thing. *Trouble.*

Chapter Four

NAOMI

I had never encountered someone like Kai before. I had known about the shifters in Sterling Meadow, but was never allowed to interact with any of them. *Ever.* I was forbidden to even glance in their direction.

But when I stood near the DJ stand searching for Barry, the only person I saw was the guy with the brown hair, big green eyes and a nose that reminded me of a Roman soldier. The surrounding people danced in slow motion.

He stared at me as if I was the only person in the world. My heart raced in my chest as the pull toward him was too great to ignore.

When his friend spoke to him and I caught hints of anger in his expression, I wanted to step away yet couldn't. Then when he turned his dark gaze on me, his expression softened, sending my heart fluttering in my ribcage.

The man approached.

I wiped damp palms on my skirt and before I could swap the file with the other hand; he stood before me.

When his eyes lingered on my breasts, I furrowed my brows. I wasn't just a body to be gawked at. Then I forgave him when he smiled; it was sweet yet seductive—sending a heated pulse directly to my core.

He was friendly and held out his hand when he greeted. The moment my hand touched his, a spark seared through my body; one I'd never experienced before and was sure he felt something too. My arms pebbled and I gasped for air.

His pupils dilated and he flinched the moment we touched. He seemed... happy. But there was something within him I couldn't place; he was different. I should be afraid of him, yet I wasn't. He wouldn't hurt me, I knew that much. And whatever he was, I felt the intense pull toward him.

After I told him my name, he kissed my hand. That gesture alone sent my blood scorching throughout my body. My cheeks heated as I thought about his soft lips on mine but I couldn't and shouldn't think of a man I hardly knew.

When a giggle tore from my lips, my desire evident. I suspected he sensed how I felt about him when his nostrils flared breathing me in.

"I didn't know men still did that," I said, curious about his true intentions, yet keeping my hand in his.

"Only the good ones," he smiled, warming me from my chest to the apex of my legs. He had an effect on me I didn't understand. It should be wrong, yet it felt right.

"I've never seen you here before," I said and felt heat rise from my chest, up my neck and cheeks. I nervously glanced away, trying to hide the fact that my body had betrayed me.

"It's my first time, but I'm glad I came," he purred.

Oh my gods. I felt giddy as I gazed up at his smooth features and mesmerizing green eyes.

One moment he was standing a few steps away, the next he stood so close I felt his warm breath on my face and chest. I didn't step away. Kai stepped closer. With his mouth near the shell of my ear, my chest rising and falling, and his hot words traveling down my neck. I shuddered in anticipation.

"I do regret not coming sooner though." He moved into my line of sight and smiled sincerely.

"Naomi!" I flinched when Michail called my name in that harsh accent. I silently cursed the bouncer for interrupting me. From the moment I started working here, I hated Sacha's most favorite *guard*.

"I have to go." I glanced at Michail then back at Kai. Through my smile I tried to portray my happiness for meeting Kai and I hoped he could tell. Although I didn't want to leave him, I had to.

I wanted Kai to know how I felt about him without sounding desperate. We just met, and it sounded ridiculous like something out of a storybook that I'd fallen so quickly for someone I hardly knew.

"Don't leave," I said, leaning in. "I will find you." As I turned away from Kai, I felt his eyes follow me like a velvety caress down my back.

My conversation was interrupted because I had to check the stock. It was a waste of my time. They needed to buy an inventory management system. It was the modern ages, and there were programs for everything. But Sacha preferred I did everything by hand because he only trusted me.

While I counted the liquor bottles, my mind drifted to Kai.

"What are you daydreaming about?" Sacha asked behind me.

I flinched at his sinister baritone and cringed at the same time. "I'm busy. What do you want?" I replied without giving him my attention.

"Michail says you've been speaking to male patrons. I'm sure I've forbidden you to interact with any of them."

"So? You still haven't given me an actual reason not to. I'm twenty-four, I can do as I please—"

"No, you can't," he boomed behind me.

His voice was so loud and frightening, it sent a shiver down my spine. I recoiled and spun around, facing him; dark shadows played against his body as he stood in the doorjamb. I didn't trust him keeping my back to him, but the sight of him standing there was no better.

"While you live under my roof, you will do as I say, Naomi. Don't make me repeat myself." The way he said my name was like nails down a chalkboard. "And the only reason I allow you to dress like that," — he pointed at my skirt and revealing blouse, — "is because I want the horny bastards to drool over you without actually touching or speaking to you."

"So it's fine for you to pimp me out to suit your needs, but the moment anyone else speaks to me then you have an issue with it. You're such a hypocrite."

"Enough!" He inched closer, towering over me. "I have already promised you to my friend's son. Do not forget about your wedding."

"Arranged wedding," I yelled. "There's no love in something forced."

"What is love, anyway?" He made a strange sound from the back of his throat. "Love is for fools. This is business. The marriage will ensure your future is comfortable."

"At what cost? My freedom?"

Sacha stood taller and glowered down at me. The single light from the store room swayed slightly and bathed his features in sinister shadows. His metallic eye glinting in the light, reminding me of cyborgs, while his blue eye filled with pent up emotion he would never divulge.

They attacked and left him for dead. Nobody knew what really happened that day. He came home, alone, and almost died. Since then, he never spoke of my mother again.

Whatever happened that night, it killed my mother and I lost a father—gaining an overbearing protector nobody knew was even my dad. I had to call him Sacha from the age of six when we first arrived in Las Vegas and travelled the country until finally settling in Sterling Meadow a couple of months ago.

"I'm only protecting you, sweet girl," he whispered, his anger tapering off. He closed his eyes and shook his head, expelling his rage. "I only want to see you happy and taken care of."

"Dad," I whispered. "I want to marry for love; not for a business arrangement. For love," I repeated, emphasizing the word love. I took his large hand in my smaller one and held it against my cheek, something I used to do as a child. The last time that happened was ten years ago. "Don't turn your back on it. There's love out there for everyone."

"Oh my child," he said in Russian. He hadn't spoken his native tongue since we left our country. He brought me into an embrace then let go, quickly glancing over his shoulder ensuring we were still alone. "I will think on it," he said in English. He let go and disappeared down the hallway, leaving me standing alone in the storeroom.

Hope built in my chest as I shuddered at the thought of

marrying someone I could never love. Maybe, just maybe, my dad would end the engagement.

When shouting erupted, I ran out to see what was going on.

Chapter Five

KAI

Lee and I approached the four men but kept our distance. Before intervening, I wanted to wait and see whether the men did anything.

I glanced around the nightclub; no bouncer in sight.

A woman screamed. I jerked my head toward her cries. The man who had spoken in line had his hand around the woman's throat and pulled her head backward, exposing her neck. It was a maneuver vampires did, but he was human. He probably did that to keep her docile.

I glimpsed at the bartender who was on the phone, hopefully calling for help.

The man said something near the woman's ear and she flinched. Her chin trembled as a lonely tear slid down the side of her face.

"Take your hands off her." Lee placed a calm hand on the man's forearm.

"Get the fuck away from me." The man jerked his chin in Lee's direction. "Malcom!"

Malcom was tall with dark features and tattoos of

snakes on both arms. He nodded, grabbed Lee's shirt and pushed him away from the other man but continued to hold on to Lee, ensuring he kept him away.

"What do you want me to do with him, Jerry?"

"Let go of me if you want to keep your hands," Lee growled.

Malcom's eyes widened. "What the——"

Before Malcom finished his sentence, Lee's hands shifted into his powerful claws and sliced off the man's hands. Malcom stumbled backward, crying as he stared in disbelief at both bloody stumps. Malcom's hands fell to the ground as another man gripped Lee's neck.

I stepped forward, punched the man away from Lee and he flew into the wall next to the bar, crumpling to the floor.

Jerry tightened his grip around the woman's throat. "What are you?" he said. His eyes widening at Lee's claws.

Lee stepped closer.

"Come near me and I'll kill her," Jerry started moving backward.

"Let go of her and we'll allow you to leave this place in one piece," I said in a low growl.

Jerry's eyes flitted from Lee to me as we advanced on him. "Get back." He pulled a switchblade from his pocket, pointing it at Lee, then at me.

The DJ killed the music.

The patrons gawked at us.

Others ran away blocking the exit.

With the surrounding commotion I didn't pay attention behind me. Pain seared down my back as the attacker repeatedly stabbed me, digging deeper into my flesh.

I cried out, followed by a hiss escaping my clenched teeth. Slowly, I turned around and faced my attacker. The man gasped and shook his head when he noticed my glowing eyes. I reached for the knife lodged in my back, pulled it out and pointed it at my assailant.

"That wasn't very nice," I said sinisterly. My tone deep and throaty as my leopard flared to the surface, desperate to shift so I could heal, but I couldn't; not yet and not here.

"I'm s-sorry, I d-didn't mean to." The man spluttered, walking backward to get away. Unfortunately for him, he didn't see the fallen bar stool and fell over it, crashing to the ground with a loud thud, followed by painful moans.

Lee glowered over the man as his claws shifted back into hands.

I caught movement out of the corner of my eye. The man who still held onto his female hostage moved farther away.

"What the hell is going on?"

I turned in the voice's direction.

Naomi stomped toward the man holding the woman, and in two swift moves she kicked his shin and relieved him of his knife. Jerry crashed to the floor, jumped up a second later using the opportunity to get away, and dashed for the exit.

"Barry!" Naomi yelled, and a different bouncer entered from the side and gripped Jerry by his neck.

Barry towered over everyone as his meaty hands squeezed, cutting Jerry's air.

"It's not me, it's them. They aren't human." Jerry managed to say through a hoarse whisper, trying in vain to get out of Barry's grip.

Naomi's eyes flitted from Jerry to Lee and noticed blood on his hands.

"You were the one holding a woman hostage," Naomi said to him, then to Barry she added. "Take him outside before Sacha gets hold of him."

She turned to face me, her eyes blazing with power as we stared at each other. I waited for her wrath, instead one side of her mouth curved upward as she said, "Thank you for helping. We rarely get those types here. Something must've happened to Mark."

"Naomi!" Barry yelled from somewhere near the exit.

Naomi ran. Lee and I followed.

As we exited, I welcomed the cool evening air as it chilled my skin. I was heating as I fought for control over my leopard. I couldn't shift now. I had to wait until we got back to the warehouse. And I didn't want Naomi to see that part of me, yet.

As we rounded the corner we stopped. In the alley lay the bouncer who managed the outside queue.

"This asshole hurt Mark," Barry said, his chest rising and falling as he fought his own anger demons.

"Is he breathing?" Naomi crouched and felt his pulse. "Oh, thank gods. He'll be fine." She stood as Mark stirred and turned her attention on Jerry. Her icy stare sent a shiver down my spine that scared and enticed me. She was a spit-fire in a skirt. I couldn't help but smirk.

In a bitter tone that only added to her charm, she said. "He deserves to go out back."

I didn't need to know what she meant, but this was a Russian nightclub and they usually dealt with things in their own special way.

Barry dragged Jerry by his neck, and no amount of kicking and fighting would break the hold Barry had on him.

"Are you okay?" Naomi touched my back. "You're bleeding," she whispered as she touched my shirt; she was so gentle, yet I felt her fingers burn my skin.

I turned to face her. We stood so close I smelled her

sweet scent, but there was something else mixed in. Fear. Adrenaline. Lust?

"I'll be fine. Just make sure that woman is okay." I barely felt the knife wound before she had mentioned it. But it stung now.

"I will."

The man who'd first called Naomi ran into the alley, aimed his gun at me, then at Lee. "Get away from them, Naomi. I watched the video. They're fucking shifters," he said, then rambled on in Russian that sounded like swear words.

"Calm down, Michail. They helped me and stopped the real bad guy from hurting one of our regulars."

"Get away or I'll call Sacha."

"Stop it." She lifted her hands and came between Michail and me. "Put that down. And stop using Sacha's name when you need me to do something. I've had enough—"

"I do what Sacha tells me to do. He asked me to fetch you and to put these fuckers in the ground."

"No! You will do no such thing. Not while I work here."

"We'll see about that."

"Enough." Naomi grabbed the gun out of his hand with such confidence I knew she could handle herself in a tricky situation. A grin split my face in two when she turned the gun on Michail.

Michail slowly raised his hands and just as quickly hit her in the face, taking back his gun. She fell backward, landing on the cold ground.

I didn't think—I reacted. Someone had hurt Naomi and I couldn't allow him to get away with his actions. He needed to be stopped. I jumped onto Michail and bit down into his muscular neck.

"Kai! No!" Naomi shrieked, trying to pull me off Michail.

"Let's go!" Lee yelled frantically.

I unclenched my jaw from Michail's tender flesh, savoring the metallic taste as I swallowed his blood and the chunk of flesh.

"Argh," Michail called out, covering the wound with one powerful hand. "I'm going to kill you, you animal."

Lee grabbed my arm, trying to pull me away from the deadly scene.

As stubborn as I was, I couldn't leave yet.

"I need to see you again," I said. "I need…" I started, realizing I couldn't leave her with only parting words. I wanted to give her something memorable. To think about when she's alone. I wanted to give her something personal… intimate.

I swallowed, wiping blood from my mouth and ran back to her. I grabbed her, one hand clasping the back of her head, the other at the small of her back, and pulled her against my body.

I kissed her, not only with my lips but with my soul. Not understanding why, I offered myself to her—not only a sliver, but my entire being.

At first, she fought against me, trying to push me away. But as my tongue teased the slit of her mouth, my hands keeping her against me, she relaxed and opened herself to me. She stopped pushing against my chest and wrapped them around my neck.

I responded by holding her tighter against my body until I felt her heart beat against my chest; beating as one. I kissed her fiercely, tangling my tongue with hers. When her tongue swept along my leopard fangs a soft moan escaped her mouth, and I swallowed it, devouring it. It sent a shiver down my spine and I savored it; wanting and needing more.

My pulse thundered in my head. Beast wanted her.

She hesitated as if sensing something—heard something.

My thoughts crashed to visions of her naked beneath me, and I had to stop. This was not the right place or the right time. I would find her again and she would be mine. I needed her to see there was more to me than just the animal.

Slowly, I pulled away from her, breaking the kiss.

I stared down at her with longing and a deep craving.

She returned the look with one of bewilderment or shock.

"Do you read?" I asked.

She stared wide eyed and eventually nodded.

Leaning forward with my lips near her neck, where her pulse throbbed, I whispered near her ear. "Meet me at the bookstore tomorrow at noon."

"We got to go." Lee pulled on my shirt.

The door banged open. Shouting erupted in Russian, followed by many footsteps.

Lee and I ran across the road, climbed into our car and sped away.

Chapter Six

KAI

There was only one bookstore in Sterling Meadow. Humans and monsters read, but not as much as they used to. Today there was more to keep everyone occupied; from electronic devices to movies while reading was only a close third. Also, why would anyone read when they could ask the source who had actually lived during those times? A monster who had lived thousands of years was the first choice, of course.

I parked farther down the street and walked the block with the park on my left, and on the other side of the street were shops.

The bookstore sat between a coffee shop, *'Alpha Coffee'*, and a clothing store. *'Alpha Coffee'* was run by Jason, a were-wolf, and it was the best coffee in town.

I sucked air over my teeth, scenting my surroundings. Remnants of last night's rain, perfume, coffee and freshly baked goods wafted in the air as I neared the coffee shop. Women exited the clothing store with bags, smiles on their faces, and no doubt an empty bank account.

The walk provided me with clarity regarding last night's

events. When Lee and I got back to the warehouse we discussed what had happened. Lee shook his head, not believing my instant attraction to Naomi was possible.

It was strange how quickly I felt all those emotions and I knew Naomi felt them, too. The touch of her hand had sent an electrical current coursing through my veins, leaving me hot and needing more; to touch her, to taste her, and to see her. But for now, all I had to hold onto was a distant memory of her which I savored with delight.

Then my thoughts crashed to the bouncer I attacked. There were consequences for my actions and I needed to make amends. And I hoped to see Naomi today to apologize.

I entered the bookstore and the smell of ink, dust and paper assaulted my senses first, relaxing my shoulders. I preferred reading books, instead of watching something mindless on TV.

I loved the thought process of the writer and what they went through as they wrote their words. How those words transformed in my imagination as I watched the book play out like a movie in my mind.

When I approached the middle aisle, a shiver slipped down my spine. The sun's rays seeped in through the blinds and splashed against her raven hair, reflecting a deep cobalt. I wasn't sure whether it was her natural hair color, but it was fit for a queen; *My queen*.

Not wanting to disturb Naomi as she read from a book; she was so engrossed with the words she didn't hear me approach. It gave me a moment to appreciate the defined shape of her nose; her smooth pale skin and rosy lips. She mumbled to herself as she read. I leaned against the high bookshelf with my right foot crossed over the left.

"I didn't think you'd come," I whispered.

A smile tugged on her lips, and she glanced up from her book. "Well, I had to know more about the stranger who caused all the trouble in my club." She shelved the book and walked away from me.

Glancing around to ensure we were alone, I stalked after her: a leopard after his prey. I'd love to pounce on her in the store so everybody could see she belonged to me. But I wouldn't.

When I reached the end of the aisle, I glanced left; nothing. When I looked right, I caught sight of her hand before she disappeared into the next aisle. I gave chase and entered the next aisle. Again, I only caught her red dress billowing behind her as she went into the next row.

When I reached the end of the row, people entered the store.

I entered the last row, stopping dead. My mouth opened in a surprised *O*.

Naomi stopped and slowly turned to face me. Her deep blue eyes smiling as her chest heaved up and down trying to catch her breath.

I neared. She backed up into the corner with her hands behind her back. She leaned her body against the wall with nowhere to go.

Her delicate fragrance wafted in the air and beneath that her desire. All I wanted to do in this moment was surround her body with mine.

I glanced at the books on the shelves and smiled. "I had no idea this was on your mind."

The lines between her eyes deepened and she read the titles of the books near her and her cheeks turned a healthy shade of pink. "This was not my intention—"

"I don't mind at all." I seductively touched my chest. "If

all you want me for is my body." I moved my hands down my body, then cupped myself.

Her neck and cheeks reddened, and her breathing labored. She rested her head against the wall, exposing her neck and smiled with hooded eyes. "You are easy on the eyes, Kai, at least buy me lunch first."

"Well," — I arched an eyebrow, — "that's not on my mind, yet," I said, grinning. "I would prefer to get to know you first." I turned to the side and lifted my elbow for her to take. "Now where would you like to go?"

Chapter Seven

NAOMI

I stared at the sexy stranger, tracing my fingertips over my lips, remembering our shared kiss. Memories of my heart racing even after he had left. But the memory of his hands on my body, his lips on mine, and his tongue exploring my mouth kept flashing before me.

I remembered how my body had heated at the apex of my thighs, a live wire of sensual energy I couldn't turn off. The only thing that had helped last night was a cold shower when I got home—three hours after that delicious moment felt like an eternity, and I wanted to revel in that heat again.

Warning bells should've gone off, I just met him, yet I felt the connection deep within. It was a feeling I simply couldn't ignore.

My cheeks heated as my heart slammed against my chest. Kai probably thought I was deprived or perverted for stopping in an aisle filled with books on sex.

The longer I stared at him, the more I relaxed. He did that to me; he calmed me without laying a finger. Glancing at his powerful hands, I ached for his touch.

A smile tugged at the corners of my mouth as I raked my gaze over his hard body. His hair stuck up in all directions like he'd fallen out of bed, but it opened his face; revealing how handsome he was. He hadn't shaved in a few weeks, but I appreciated the look—it suited him. He wore dark jeans with sneakers and a heavy metal t-shirt. He was slightly taller than me, much taller if I kicked off my heels.

I swallowed hard as he touched himself. I thought about removing an item of clothing, one piece at a time, and throwing it at him to make him squirm. But there was a time and place for everything and doing anything like that in a book shop was tacky.

"You are easy on the eyes, Kai, at least buy me lunch." I wanted him to know that I was interested in him without coming across as desperate. It was a skill I hadn't mastered yet.

"Well," — he arched an eyebrow, — "that's not on my mind, yet," he grinned. "I would prefer to get to know you first." He lifted his elbow for me to take. "Now where would you like to go?"

I hesitated at first, glancing around. When I was sure nobody was watching, I slipped my arm through his.

Chapter Eight

KAI

Once outside, Naomi became shy walking beside me. I grabbed her hand reassuringly and her cheeks glowed. When I asked her a question she shrugged, answering quietly. Her hand was a little clammy, and she giggled nervously.

She came across as timid or reserved but then I remembered how she handled herself last night and shook it off to being in my company for the first time and we just needed to get to know each other. Whatever it was, I wouldn't give up on her easily.

At first, Naomi had said she wouldn't mind eating at the coffee shop, but I didn't want to—not for our first date. I wanted a venue where we could talk privately. The only place I was comfortable enough was one of Léon's places that catered specifically for shifters.

When I mentioned this to Naomi, she stopped walking and shook her head. "I can't, Kai."

"Why?"

She bit her lip, unable to give me a straight answer. She

seemed to fumble over her words, then settled that she couldn't be seen in the company of half-beasts.

"Um, Naomi, you know I'm one, right?"

We were halfway to my car and stopped in the middle of the sidewalk, people rushing past us trying to get to their destinations.

She nodded.

"Help me understand. I won't hurt you. And my people will know you're with me." I squeezed her hand reassuringly. "I want you to see there's nothing to worry about when you're among my kind." I didn't ask her whether she knew which animal I was, I wanted her to ask first.

As if reading my mind, she asked the burning question.

"Which were-animal are you?" she swallowed hard and stared with wide eyes. The sun was out, but dark clouds formed and swept low over the sky. Her blue-black hair darkened and her cerulean-blue eyes glowed when the sun peaked between clouds then casting her in shadows as the clouds moved on.

"I don't want to discuss this out here." I surveyed our surroundings. We were alone, but I didn't want to tell her *here*. "Come with me." I led her to my car. "If you feel uncomfortable at any time, I promise you we can leave. I want to show you everything there is to know about me and let you decide. I don't want us to start off with any secrets between us."

I opened the car door for her, watching her sit down inside my car felt natural like she belonged beside me. It was absolutely crazy I felt that way. *Was it all too soon?*

As I started the car and pulled into traffic, out of the corner of my eyes, she kept squeezing her hands. I reached for her. She didn't flinch when I held her hand and brought it near my mouth and kissed her knuckles.

There were things I wanted to tell her but it might scare her off. If what I said scared her, we would return to her car. It was now or never; I only lived once with burning words desperate to come out.

"Naomi," — my heart rate kicked up a notch and fire ignited in my veins, — "I know we're moving fast. I know I might have scared you last night, and you taking the chance to meet me today thrilled me. But there's just something I can't deny—"

"I feel it too." She squeezed my hand and nodded as she stared at me. "I feel it in my chest." She clutched her other hand to her heart. "And somehow, I know you won't harm me. I can't explain it. It's like a fairy tale, but I'm not a kid and I know this isn't that, but it's different. It's real. You know?"

I smiled warmly, understanding what she meant, and we drove the rest of the way in comfortable silence.

Chapter Nine

NAOMI

As a child I was taught to fear supernatural's of any kind. Sacha had said I could only trust him, along with those who helped run the club. But it frustrated me how the others at the club tried to dominate me even though I was their superior.

Staring at Kai, I knew he'd keep me safe. It was hard to describe but it felt as though I knew him my whole life. That we were somehow meant to be together. But fairy tales didn't exist—I wasn't a child. Yet, what I felt for Kai was real.

As much as I wanted to know more about his kind, I was afraid Sacha would find out. If he knew about Kai, or how he made me feel, Sacha would kill him for fear of losing his business contract with the man he had promised me to. Sacha may have said he would think on it, but he hadn't cancelled it yet. There was still a chance he would force me into a loveless marriage.

If Kai found out about the arranged marriage, he wouldn't want to see me again. I doubted any man would risk his life to be with me; I wasn't worth the risk—no matter what he thought or how he felt. Our feelings may not even be real.

I realized Kai was a shifter when I saw his claws last night, but I wasn't afraid. I wanted to touch them and hoped he would change into his beast.

"Which were-animal are you?" I asked, fearing the question more than the answer. A nervousness swept through my core that somehow, I already knew what he was. *A leopard*. I had no way of truly knowing just by his claws alone, but deep within I was right.

When Kai said he would tell me but not here, I reluctantly agreed to see the place he had mentioned, but would remain cautious.

I listened intently to Kai's words and allowed him to hold my hand as we strolled to his car. He was the perfect gentleman closing the door for me. And I continued listening to him as he drove.

"I feel it too," I said with a burning desire. "I feel it in my chest." I clutched my hand to my chest. "And somehow, I know you won't harm me. I can't explain it. It's like a fairy tale, but I'm not a kid and I know this isn't that, but it's different. It's real. You know?"

Kai smiled warmly in understanding, leaving my heart swelling for this kitty I hardly knew.

We drove the rest of the way in comfortable silence.

Chapter Ten

KAI

Ten minutes later I pulled up the dirt road that led to a secluded lodge only for shifters. It was a place where the WAA got together monthly to discuss issues, and it was open all day and night. It was a place for were-animals to eat and shift if needed—they hardly did, but the lodge had accommodation for those new fledglings who couldn't control their beast quite yet.

There were a handful of vehicles parked near the lodge as we stopped. I tasted dew in the air with the surrounding forest; pines and wet dirt. I opened the car door for Naomi and reached for her hand. She didn't hesitate and slipped her hand into mine. She was warm to the touch and moved closer as we traversed up the stairs to the entrance.

The smell of her floral scent awakened a need within and a low growl rumbled through my chest and out my lips, baring my emerging fangs.

Naomi stopped and stared up at me, she'd heard my call and responded by not running away. She wasn't afraid. She was curious and stayed by my side. She stood before me, her hand raising to my mouth. I curled my lips, baring my fangs. She touched them.

"Is this the first time you're seeing someone like me?" I wanted to step away from her, to keep my distance, but I didn't. If she could face me, someone she hardly knew, then I could allow her to look at me, and touch every inch of my body if she chose.

I expected her to run away, but she didn't. She was as inquisitive as a child; with her left palm pressed against my chest, her right hand near my mouth and her body pressed up against mine. I stared into her eyes even though her attention was on my fangs. I noted the pulse on the main vein in her neck and my fangs extended to their full length.

She didn't gasp as she watched, fixated on my sharp teeth. "They're beautiful." Her eyes shifted to mine and added. "You're beautiful."

My smile split my face in two. I loved hearing her say that but I was more interested in her and why I'd never seen her before. Sterling Meadow was a relatively small town, and it was my business to know most of the residents yet I knew nothing about her.

"Why haven't I seen you around?"

She shrugged. "I've been working to get the club up and running. We've only been here a few months and I had a lot to do."

I nodded my understanding but I had more questions. "And why is it you haven't seen were-animals before?"

She stepped backward and averted her eyes.

I reached for her chin and lifted it, wanting to see her eyes. "Why hide?"

"It's my f—I mean, Sacha. He is very protective…" she choked on her words and shook her head. "I can't." She continued shaking her head.

"Do you want to leave?" I asked with concern. I didn't want her to leave, but I'd take her to her car if she desired. The last thing I wanted to do was force her to stay. Even if it hurt to let go.

"Oh, no! I don't want to leave. It's just... I can't explain, not yet." She spun around and opened the door.

Chapter Eleven

NAOMI

I entered the venue, it was pleasant enough with lots of leather booths lining one wall, tables and chairs in the center, a bar on the other side with a kitchen in the back. It smelled like leather, food, and animals. There were hallways that led left and right to the various bathrooms. My arms pebbled when I saw the arrow pointing down to the den.

"What's down there?" I asked.

Kai stopped behind me, his larger hand still holding mine. He squeezed gently. With a smile he added, "Sometimes a young shifter can't control their beast. We take them down there until they recover. There's food for them and they can sleep it off, safely."

He squeezed my hand reassuringly and it comforted me.

"This is a safe space for shifters to come and enjoy themselves. Nobody wants to get hurt. It never used to be so mild, but times have changed. Each of the were-animal numbers are dwindling."

When I knitted my brows, he explained.

"There have been attacks from witches. Newcomers in

Sterling Meadow have caused havoc and killed a few beasts. With this latest disease forcing everyone to wear masks, good shifters have died. We are not immortal like vampires, we are still very much half-human. We're stronger, live longer, and lead healthy lives. But we can die, and with our numbers decreasing, we're trying to keep everyone safe. There's only a handful of shifters born per year, and while others want the change willingly our numbers remain low. But what's frowned upon is attacking humans and forcing the change upon them. If they ever attacked anyone, the WAA investigates the crime and finds those accountable, and punishable by death."

"I had no idea all of this was going on." I gripped his arm tighter and leaned into his shoulder. "But I want to know everything about you and what goes on."

Kai led me to a private booth in a corner and the server came over with menu's.

"Glad to have you back, Kai. Is the Master keeping you and Lee out of trouble?"

Kai chuckled. "Hey, Delores. Yeah, Léon keeps both our asses out of trouble. This is Naomi."

"Haven't seen you before, hun. Welcome to the family," Delores beamed at me, handing us a menu each.

Kai ordered us drinks.

"I'll be back to get your food order," Delores said, leaving us alone.

I exhaled a shaky breath, and relaxed my shoulders. I'd long forgotten his growl and display of fangs outside. When I first noticed Kai's fangs emerge, instead of feeling afraid, I wanted to touch them. He intrigued me.

And when he mentioned coming here, I was apprehensive but now that I was here, it wasn't that bad. There were other patrons enjoying their lunch, but I didn't feel threatened or afraid—like Sacha had taught me to be. He had said that all were-animals were the devil's spawn and I should stay away. That I only trusted my own kind.

I smiled glancing around the venue; the place had a familiar homey feeling to it.

"I like the place," I finally said and glanced at the menu. "And they have quite a variety of *food* here." I didn't think were-animals ate normal cooked food.

A strange sound came from the back of Kai's throat. It wasn't a growl or a cough; it was more like a strangled laugh. "The only time we eat raw meat is downstairs while we're in our beast. The rest of the time, we're just like you," he smiled sincerely. "Oh, and every full moon we hunt together as a pack and feast as we celebrate."

I stared wide eyed at Kai, then quickly glanced down at the menu. I hoped he wasn't silently judging me for our differences, or my lack of knowledge. I exhaled sharply and tried to relax again, but my mind busied with questions I wanted to ask.

"Who do you hunt?" I asked meekly.

"Only wild animals," he grinned. "Like I said before, things have changed. Shifters have mellowed out, well, most of us have. Do you see something you like?" He jerked his chin at my menu.

Delores gave us our drinks and we ordered something to eat.

When Delores left, there was a comfortable silence, then Kai asked a question. "So, tell me more about where you're from." He sipped on his beer, considering me. He knew where I was from because of my slight Russian accent, but it was kind of him to ask.

"Russia," — I tucked a loose strand of hair behind my ear, — "I was quite young when we came here. My dad ensured I was home schooled in English and Russian by the best tutors, and then I started working for him." I cringed as the words flew out of my mouth. There was something about Kai that I wanted to share every detail of my life. It didn't matter if he knew, he would eventually find out. And he had said there should be no secrets between us.

"So, Sacha is your father?" Kai asked carefully and sat back.

I nodded. "He doesn't want anyone to know," I said with an imploring look.

"Don't worry, your secret is safe with me." He held his hand out.

I hesitated at first. Kai wasn't trying to do anything other than hold my hand. Once I realized this, I placed my hand in his.

"I never knew my parents. I was an orphan for as long as I could remember. After running away from every single home, I joined the military. There…" — he combed his fingers through his hair, — "after my attack I became something better, stronger, and something I never thought I would actually like being. And for you to still have a parent who cares so much is wonderful." When I opened my mouth, he held up his hand to stop me from talking. "Yes, he is overbearing, but he loves you. One can never take that away from a father who means well."

"You're right, but…" I swallowed my words and downed my drink. "He would kill you if he knew what you are."

"Does that mean I'll see you again?" he grinned. My smile widened. I hoped to see him again but didn't want to say it out loud first.

"Well, in that case, let him try." Kai winked darkly. My cheeks heated.

"I'm serious, Kai. He will kill you."

"I know. And it's okay, Naomi, really. I can't change his mind about shifters. If he ever finds out about me, all I can do is introduce myself and take it from there, but I'll never regret meeting you. You're worth the risk."

It meant so much to hear him say that, but I didn't want him getting hurt.

"That means you can never come to the club. Ever."

His throat moved up and down as he swallowed. He let go of my hand, sat back again and stared at me.

"I don't think I can do that. I need to see you more often and if that means at the club, then that's where I'm going."

"You bit Michail. He and Barry know what you look like and that you are a shifter. They will tell Sacha. He probably has someone looking for me already." The thought crossed my mind and my body chilled. I told Sacha I wanted to buy clothing and should've been back home already. Knowing Sacha, he would send Barry to bring me back home. Sacha usually sent Michail but he was recovering.

"Maybe we need to speak privately with your dad before he hears stories from his men."

I shook my head as my eyes stung. I became overwhelmed with emotions, not knowing how to react in front of him.

I raised my hand for the server and asked for another drink. I needed to calm my nerves, if only for a few minutes.

Kai sat patiently and silently, watching me intently.

I felt uncomfortable. It wasn't because of him, but my reactions toward him. My feelings felt foreign and left me unsure about myself. It should've felt wrong to feel this way for him yet it felt right all the same.

When the server brought my drink, Kai politely asked for another beer. Now I was rude for not waiting for him to ask for another drink.

"We can drink an entire keg of this and not feel a buzz," he said, finishing his beer.

That caught my attention and relieved he'd changed the subject. I stared at him, sipping on my second martini. "Oh, how much do you have to drink before you feel anything?"

"Oh, about a bottle or two of Tequila," he said with a sharp grin. "Our metabolism is quick, that stuff hardly does anything to us. But what gets to us is usually the stuff from a witch's brew," he smiled again.

My heart skipped a beat before it pounded against my ribs. Kai made me *feel* everything. I felt his words against my skin, his warm smile against my face, and his gaze against my body. Everything about him swirled around me like a comforting blanket. And when he smiled, my heart skipped a beat. But there were a few things I needed to know.

"It's strange…" I swallowed, trying to find the right words to how I felt. "I feel…" I touched my chest near my heart. "I'm only human. Yet—"

His eyes brightened. "Yet you feel the pull?"

I nodded, a thin smile playing on my lips. I'd heard stories of those fated to spend an eternity together would feel an intense attraction. I wondered whether what I felt was that. But it couldn't be since I was human. I was under the impression only were-animals were fated mates.

"But I'm human."

"That's just it. I've heard of others finding human mates, although not often. I don't know what we have and I don't want to put a label on it. All I'm asking is, let's see where this takes us?"

The rest of the time we spoke about the things we wanted out of life. Kai wanted to travel, and I wanted to sail. Kai wanted to have his own coffee shop filled with books, and I offered to do his accounting. When I said that, his face lit up highlighting the emerald sparkle in his eyes.

Our banter continued while we ate and drank.

I felt Kai's heated gaze on me throughout our conversation and all I thought about was touching him. A burning desire raged within and I ached to strip naked against him.

My phone vibrated in my bag, tearing me away from my wanton thoughts. The insistent silent ringing against my leg did nothing to make me want to answer it. I knew who it was and why they were calling. *'Naomi, where are you?', 'Naomi, what are you doing?', 'Naomi, you need to wait for the delivery.', 'Naomi, I need you to do everything in this club.'*

I exhaled frustratingly and pushed my bag to the side so that I didn't feel it anymore.

When the restaurant darkened, it was time for me to leave—like Cinderella running away. I had to work soon and couldn't hide away from my father even though I wanted to. It physically pained me to think those thoughts, but I couldn't stay. Sacha would send Barry or one of the others; if they weren't already here.

"We have to go," I said sadly, reaching for my bag. "I have to work tonight."

"I'll get you to your car." He smiled warmly, making my heart rate speed up again.

"Promise me you won't come tonight."

"I can't promise you that."

"Promise me, Kai. Sacha will kill you."

"I'll think about it." He grinned.

Chapter Twelve

KAI

After Naomi climbed into my car and I closed the door, I felt a heavy weight against my back. The air snapped and the ground shook as someone stalk behind me. I spun around before the assailant wrapped his meaty hands around my neck.

"No!" Naomi cried, opening the car door but I kicked it closed before she had the chance.

"Stay inside." I pointed at her, she nodded reluctantly.

I faced Barry, the tall Russian made entirely of muscles, with white hair cut short, white eyebrows and piercing blue eyes. I sniffed the air and caught an odor — a bear shifter. This wasn't going to end well for either of us. Those fuckers fought dirty.

Barry arched an eyebrow as if sensing my thoughts and with a meaty finger beckoned me closer.

"Do you want to dance, Barry?" I taunted, stepping away from the car.

"I've always wanted to snap a leopard in two," he grinned a toothy smile.

"No!" Naomi said.

"I told you to stay in the car."

"Yeah, let the lady save the pussy cat."

That was it. I hated fighting, but loved nothing more than smacking this guy around. Without warning I pounced on the bigger man wrapping my arms around his neck in a choke hold. Barry gripped my arms, trying to release the hold but I had mastered this.

Because I wasn't as large as other shifters, I learned to do things differently and still win a fight if backed into the corner. One of those was the element of surprise, and the other, the choke hold to render any shifter motionless.

As much as I wanted to snap Barry's neck, Naomi was watching. I couldn't kill anyone with her around, and especially if she knew the brute.

Barry gasped for breath, gripping my arms trying to pry me off but it wasn't working.

"Tell your boss I'm not going anywhere and I will see Naomi. Nod if you understand."

Barry fell to his knees. His animal rippled beneath his skin, itching for release. The moment I let go he would shift.

"Do you know he's a bear?"

"Sacha hires a few shifters to help out at the club." Naomi approached.

"Stay back, Naomi," I growled, wanting her safe; if she came closer Barry could shift and hurt her.

"Please don't kill him," she pleaded for the shifters life.

"He's tough, Naomi, I have to snap his neck to stop him. I just need to subdue him so he doesn't hurt me. But more importantly I don't want him hurting you."

I didn't want her getting hurt. I didn't know what Barry wanted to do but knew it wasn't pleasant. And neither me nor beast wanted Naomi hurt.

"Now Barry, I'm going to let go and you are going to let us step away. Nod if you understand."

Barry nodded and collapsed to the ground, his face eating dirt.

Slowly, I unclasped my arms from Barry's neck and stood.

"Get in the car," I yelled, rushing to the car and climbed in. I hit the gas the moment she was strapped in the car.

"He knows... he knows... he knows..." Naomi cried into her hands the moment we were on the open road. "I can't believe he had me followed. He's going to kill you." She glanced at me and my heart sank at her expression. She seemed so fragile yet all she worried about was my safety.

"He can come for me. I'll be ready," I said, my tone cold.

Chapter Thirteen

KAI

After the altercation with Barry, I didn't want to leave Naomi alone with them. Beast and I wanted to protect her and against my better judgement, I needed to ensure her safety while she worked.

"You don't have to stay." I pulled open the security gate that led to the basement door. We found a weak spot at the club not under guard or being used.

Lee shook his head. "You know I'll never leave you when you need me the most. I still think you're an idiot, though. But that's why we're friends." He punched my shoulder.

"Ow!"

"That's for falling in love, you freakin' idiot. Now step aside." Lee pushed me to one side, inserted the lock pick, did his magic, and the door clicked opened. "It would've been easier to just rip the door off its hinges—"

"But then they'll know we're here."

Lee swatted my chest. "I'm not the idiot like you." He pushed open the door.

I smiled; we'd been through so much together and I was incredibly lucky to have him as my best friend. He wasn't handsome, yet always managed to be the first to speak with the ladies. And he was one of the most genuine people I'd ever met. We were brothers bound by animal and the best of friends.

I entered the dank room behind Lee. Our cat-eyes adjusting to the darkness.

They packed the basement with crates of unused glasses, old or broken chairs and a broken bar counter. A rat scurried past.

We stepped over rodent traps and feces and tried not to breathe in the stench of damp wood and liquor. We maneuvered through the broken furniture until we reached the steps leading to the offices.

After I dropped Naomi at her vehicle this afternoon, I phoned Blaire Thorne, a monster assassin, for information. Within minutes she sent me the blueprints for the nightclub along with the renovations they had done. She also warned me not to mess with the Russians. And she had learned of shifters threatened with a new type of bullet that could seriously harm us and advised I be careful.

As much as I hated admitting that breaking into a nightclub was a stupid idea I did it anyway. And if Sacha and his bodyguards had those bullets, I would still take a chance. That's how much Naomi meant to me.

The plan was to slip inside the club undetected, then sneak to the dance floor and somehow surprise Naomi. I hoped she was around otherwise I would blend in with the shadows against the walls until I saw her.

Lee glanced my way when we reached the door leading to the offices. "Can you hear someone speaking Russian in that office over there," — I nodded. Lee thumbed to his right, — "And it's clear that side." I nodded again, confirming what he heard was correct. Lee slowly turned the doorknob, and it squeaked opened.

We entered the quiet corridor, avoiding the offices to the left. Then as quietly as we could, we snuck through the bar area and entered the club through the door Naomi had used last night. The music was loud, the air hot. I fanned my shirt but it didn't help.

We casually approached the bar as if we owned the place and I didn't think anyone noticed us.

I pulled on my beanie, hopefully masking my appearance as I ordered Tequila shots from the barman. We downed two shots each then canvassed the room.

"I don't see her." Lee leaned against the wall and tipped his black Fedora at a female who'd winked at him.

I elbowed him. "Don't attract attention to yourself."

"I can't help it if the ladies find me irresistible," he grinned. "And besides, I need to keep myself occupied when your lady eventually shows."

The door we had just used opened, catching my attention. When I saw Naomi, my sleeping beast awakened. My eyes raked up her body and something within stirred. My hands burned with desire to touch her. For now, I stole glimpses of her.

She approached the DJ, whispered in his ear, then crossed the dancefloor. She didn't search the area because she'd told him not to come, therefore wasn't expecting me. But I couldn't stay away.

I cocked my head to the side and frowned. She didn't wear so much makeup last night. I caught Lee's attention and pointed at her. He nodded and sat near the bar.

I maneuvered through the crowd, and just as she was about to slip past me, I caught her elbow. She gasped as she glanced at the person grabbing her and was about to pull out of my grip. Her tough expression softened when she realized it was me, but then her lips went into a straight line.

"Kai! I told you not to come. What's wrong with you?" She checked to see whether anyone was around and guided us into the coatroom.

"Why are you wearing so much makeup?" I growled and thumbed her cheek. Beneath the heavy layer of base was a bruise. "Who did this to you?" My beast pushed against me, eager to kill everyone who had hurt her.

"Please don't cause trouble." Naomi pushed away from me and the coats to stand deeper inside the room. "Sacha isn't happy you bit Michail and almost strangled Barry. And he's certainly unhappy about you taking me to the shifter place."

"Did he do this?" I carefully touched her bruised cheek but she swatted my hand away.

"Please—" she shook her head. "Don't make things worse."

"Who hit you, Naomi?" I growled low and my fangs emerged.

Naomi pressed her hand against my chest and shook her head. "I've calmed him down, and so must you. If he finds out you're here, he'll kill you." Her eyes watered. "Please, you need to leave. Now. Promise me you'll go."

I didn't want to leave Naomi with men who hit women; especially my woman. Although I hadn't claimed this beauty yet, it filled me with rage that men didn't blink at hitting a woman.

My nostrils flared as I controlled beast. He wanted to tear down this establishment, brick by brick, and make those who'd hurt her pay. But he couldn't. For her, he wouldn't.

I saw the conflicting desperation in her eyes. She didn't want Sacha hurt, but she didn't want me hurt either.

She pleaded with her eyes, and the touch of her delicate hand burned my chest. I wouldn't do anything that brought her harm, but I wouldn't leave her alone either. I'd ensure she arrived home safely and would do so every evening if I had to.

I exhaled sharply, taking her hands in mine and kissed the top of them as I steadied his breathing. Beast growled in my head and I brought her in for an embrace.

"I'll leave, but I will wait for you outside. I will escort you home where you will pack a bag and stay with me." The words stunned me as they flew out of my mouth and realized I really wanted her staying with me. I wanted to share my space with her.

If she was the one for me, I'd do everything to make her mine.

"I don't need saving, Kai." She pulled out of my arms. "I'm not a princess you need to rescue from a tower—"

"That's not what I meant, Naomi. But you need to know you have options, and I'm one of them. I'm not saying move in with me but you have a place to stay until you find your feet. Besides, a man should never hit a woman, unless it's in battle and she wields a larger sword."

Naomi bit her lip, pressed her back against the wall and closed her eyes; after a moment she opened them, the blue brightening her face.

"I know it's unhealthy for me to continue living with my father and working here, but I'm afraid if I leave…" She swallowed hard. "If I leave…" She tried again "Something might happen to Sacha. There are things you don't know."

"Like what?" I asked and for the first time since meeting, doubt crept in. A sudden surge of darkness wrapped its tendrils around my heart, leaving me afraid. I wiped clammy palms on my jeans but the thought of the unknown gnawed at me.

A cascade of emotions washed over Naomi's face as she fought what to say.

I didn't like it.

"Tell me everything. I need to know," I said softly, not wanting to scare her, even though anger raged inside.

"They have promised me to someone else." She rambled, averting her eyes.

An angry burst of emotion flooded me but I couldn't show her how the news upset me. I understood she had a life before we met. If she was promised to someone, I needed to understand more about the circumstances surrounding it.

I stared down at her but she avoided eye contact, she seemed conflicted. Touching her chin with my index finger, I lifted her jaw so she could meet my eyes. I smiled tenderly as her tears flowed.

"I don't mind the competition, Naomi."

"But that's—"

"No,"— I shook my head,— "we will figure it out. Do you love this other guy?"

"No, I haven't even met him yet."

"Okay, even better. So this is business?"

"Yes."

I exhaled and fury escaped with the breath. This I could handle. There were no emotions attached, only a business transaction. I hated the thought that even in today's times someone could still be forced into an arranged marriage whether it was for family reasons, or for business.

I kissed the tip of her nose, then delicately planted a kiss on her lips to soothe her nerves. My heart raced inside my chest and I felt her heart beat against my arm as I cupped her face.

I sensed her uneasiness.

"Do you want to marry this person?"

She shook her head and mumbled, "No. Absolutely not."

"What do you want?" I asked carefully. If she told me she didn't want me, I'd let her go, reluctantly. I would never force myself upon her to spare my own feelings. She had to be in control of what she wanted and she had to be up front about it. It would be difficult to let go after finally finding someone who made my inner beast stir, and I was falling for her... *hard*. But... if I had to fight for her, I would to the death.

My heart felt like it stopped when she opened her mouth to answer. She seemed nervous, hesitant.

"I want you."

My smile broadened, and my heart fluttered. I grazed her bottom lip with my thumb then kissed her with a fiery passion. I pressed her against the wall with my hard body. The heat from her engulfed me and I wanted her now. I wanted her skin against mine. I moved my hands to her waist, down her thigh and lifted her skirt. Her soft skin hot to the touch.

Her hands found my stomach, and she moaned in our kiss.

My smile widened and kissed harder, bruising her lips.

"I want you now," I growled near her ear and watched the hairs stand up near her neck. I kissed down the tender area near her collarbone. She smelled so good, her floral scent and her arousal; musk, tangy and a little sweet.

I pushed my hips against hers so she could feel how hard she made me, and her hands fumbled with my belt.

She froze when someone opened the door, hangers clanked against the steel rod and the door closed again.

Frustrated, I stopped and pushed away from her.

"As much as I want to ravage you now, to caress, kiss, and lick every inch of you I would rather wait. I want to take my time kissing every inch of your naked body. Lick you inside and out and take my time making you scream my name. I don't want to rush it, and not here."

One side of my mouth curved upward in a sly smile. I leaned forward and our lips touched one last time. "I'll see you after work, babe. What time do you finish?"

Naomi swallowed, licked her lips and opened her eyes. A smile flitted across her face. "At one. I've asked for an early night."

A low growl escaped my lips. I stepped backward and breathed in her scent across my teeth, savoring her smell. "We're in the midnight blue Camaro," I said and kissed her temple before leaving.

Chapter Fourteen

NAOMI

Oh my gods, what did I just do? And in the coatroom. I thought as I fixed my blouse and skirt. When I glanced in the mirror, I neatened my hair and tied it in a low ponytail. There was something missing. A quick glance on the floor and I didn't remember dropping my clipboard or cellphone. I picked them up, sighed with relief that nobody discovered us in the small room, and exited.

I timed five minutes after Kai had left before opening the coatroom door. I checked both sides before exiting but stopped, standing in the doorjamb I couldn't remember what I was doing before Kai distracted me with his lips, his hands, and his body.

I swallowed hard, remembering where his hands had touched only moments ago; the swell of my breasts and the apex of my thighs. I quivered in delight. My smile stretched across my face as I traversed down the short hallway, reading the sheet on my clipboard but not concentrating on any of the words.

Beers. That's where I was going. But I needed Mark's help with the delivery.

Once the cool autumn air kissed my still hot flesh, my heated thoughts cooled, and I was once again able to focus on my job.

The line outside was short and Mark was his usual stoic self.

After last night's excitement, Sacha had ordered more bodyguards. He didn't want to take any chances with trouble makers, nor did he want other shifters entering his nightclub again.

And with Barry trying to attack Kai earlier, Sacha had been in a foul mood when I had arrived home to change for work. He had yelled at me, followed by a slap. Usually, I didn't bruise from a slap, but I'd lost my footing and had hit the counter with my cheek.

Sacha had apologized, again, with nervous eyes on my bruised cheek. He then ordered me to cover up with makeup.

This was the last time. I loved my father, but I wouldn't be around for there to be a next time. I was done with my father's business; done with his overprotectiveness. Enough was enough.

And I instructed Sacha to stay out of my personal life and ordered him to end the business transaction. I didn't want to marry him.

Naturally, Sacha was not pleased. He had stormed out of the kitchen, leaving me to pick up the pieces once again.

I tapped on the bodyguard's shoulder. "Mark, can you help with the side door, please? We have a delivery."

"Yeah, sure," Mark nodded, then turned to his partner. "Thomas, nobody goes in until I get back." He arched an eyebrow when he saw the bruise on my cheek but said nothing.

Thomas nodded, folded his meaty arms across his broad chest and stood guard. The patrons waiting in line were quiet as church mice with soft murmurs in the far back. I wondered whether news had traveled about last night's fight.

Mark opened the side entrance while we waited a few minutes for the van to reverse. The driver climbed out to unlock the back doors of the van.

I'd ordered extra cases of beers and some kegs. Sometimes we ran low at events, making my job difficult. At least now we had extra.

The men wheeled the crates inside the basement while I moved the broken furniture to one side making space. A light caught my eye. I glanced up coming face-to-face with two sets of glowing cat's eyes. Kai. When another set of eyes came into view, I knew it was his friend, Lee.

Mark approached with a crate. I couldn't allow him to see Kai and Lee so I spun around, blocking his view.

"Out of my way, Naomi," Mark moaned.

I side-stepped and glanced over my shoulder, darkness greeted me. I exhaled a shaky breath, relieved they were hidden.

"What's up with you?" Mark asked, coming in behind me.

"Nothing. Is that it?"

"Yep. I signed for the delivery and he just pulled away," he said, surveying the basement. "We need to sort this shit out."

"I can arrange it for tomorrow. Perhaps get someone to bring their truck and we can load the broken furniture."

"Or I can do it. My truck should be big enough."

"Great, then we don't have to pay extra for removal." I headed for the exit. "You can fetch the key from me tomorrow?"

"Yeah sure," Mark hesitated as he stared at a dark corner. After a moment he grunted, turned and followed me out.

I had to lock Kai and Lee inside. Mark ensured I did it properly. After my afternoon get-away with Kai and Sacha finding out about my whereabouts, everyone was watching my every move. One slip-up and they'd tell Sacha before I could utter a 'no'. And if I didn't lock the door, Mark would know something was wrong.

I turned the key and it locked, pocketing the key chain. I walked beside Mark as we headed back to the entrance.

If Kai could break-in, I was sure he could get out again.

Chapter Fifteen

KAI

The clock in Lee's 2010 Camaro showed it was almost two in the morning. Naomi said she finished after one. Something must've happened. I reached for the door handle.

"Don't, dude. You go in there and they will skin you alive. You saw the bear, once he shifts, he will eat you."

I leaned back into the seat. "I know." I exhaled an annoyed breath.

"Then take your hand off the door handle."

I opened my mouth to reply when the staff entrance door opened. Naomi wore a long black coat, and her dark hair flowed neatly on her shoulders. She didn't bother looking around for the midnight blue Camaro; she walked straight toward them, even though they'd parked in the shadows in the corner of the parking lot.

"Start the car." I climbed out, holding the door open for her.

I smiled when she neared. She wrapped her arms round my neck and kissed me. She smelled of strawberries. When she broke the kiss, I wiped my lips, My hand sticky from whichever chapstick she had used.

She grinned knowingly.

Since only toddlers could sit in the back seat. I opted to share the front seat and climbed in first while she squealed when I pulled her onto my lap.

"I've never driven in one of these before." She held onto my neck, resting her head against mine as I held her tightly against my body.

There was no way to use the seatbelt. Instead, I'd keep her safe by protecting her with my body and held her closer.

"Hold on," Lee said and pulled away from the curb.

Naomi molded against me. It felt foreign yet comfortable.

"Was everything okay?" I whispered against her head.

"Hmm."

"Are you tired?"

"Uh-huh. Where are we going?" she asked sleepily.

"My place?" I asked carefully. Even though I said we would take her home first I didn't want to risk it. If Sacha had already hit her, me being there to whisk her away would cause another rift and I didn't want her getting hurt again.

She smiled against my neck. "Perfect."

Something loosened within my core as I held her close to my body. I never wanted to let her go.

I spoke softly near the shell of her ear, but she didn't answer. She'd fallen asleep against me and I held her tighter.

The ride to the warehouse was quiet. Nobody had followed

us from the nightclub, but that didn't mean Sacha had sent no one after her.

Lee parked in the garage and locked up while I carried my precious cargo through the warehouse toward my room.

"Shout if you need anything. I'll let Jude and Flynn know we have a guest and they need to behave."

"Yeah, thanks, man. Catch you later. And Lee, thanks for coming along."

"Sure thing." Lee winked and headed toward the kitchen.

I kicked my bedroom door closed and relief washed over me; my bedroom was tidy. I hadn't planned on bringing her here, but when I held her in my arms in the cloakroom, I wanted her here. Things were moving quickly, but it felt like the right thing to do.

I gently lay her down on my bed. When I sat up, her smiling blue eyes met mine.

"Hey sleepy-head."

Naomi sat up, threw her leg over my lap and straddled me. Before I responded, she pressed her lips against mine.

My hands roamed her body but there was too much clothing. I pulled on her blouse, fumbling with the buttons, frustrated I ripped the blouse off her body. Buttons popped and flew across the room. I kissed her shoulder and blew against her skin, smirking as the tiny hairs on her body rose, making her giggle.

Next, I fiddled with her skirt, opting to tear it from her body than to continue struggling with the zipper; leaving streams of the material dangling off the bed. I didn't hesi-tate removing my clothing and within seconds we were lying face-to-face, skin-to-skin.

Naomi covered her mouth as she laughed. "Wow, okay. That's never happened before." Her stomach muscles bunched as she giggled, then her laughter slowly faded as her eyes locked onto mine.

"Have you done it before?" I asked carefully. With her sheltered life, I wasn't sure if she knew what to expect. If she didn't, I wanted to be extra careful. Hurting her was the last thing I wanted, or worse, scaring her away.

Her laughter subsided completely and said seriously. "Only a few times, with the same guy. It was an awful experience, and I hated every minute."

Oh, boy.

"I must ask, to be sure. That you want to—"

"Absolutely," she said, pushing against me until she was on top. Her lips caressed my skin as she left delicate kisses on my neck. She kissed down my body and grazed her teeth on a nipple, making me hiss. I enjoyed the sensual pain she inflicted.

I gripped her hips but had to let go as she continued leaving soft kisses down my body. She kissed and licked my honed body, scraping her fingernails down my abdomen. When she reached my hip bone, she hit the sensitive spots that drove me crazy. I stiffened, trying my best not to ravage her, instead allowing her the freedom to do whatever she wanted on my body. If she'd been with the same guy and it was awful, I would leave her to make up her own mind to see what she wanted to do.

When she found what she was looking for, she sat up. "Wow, I don't know whether that would fit," she grinned. "But I can try."

As I wanted to respond, she grabbed my shaft with both warm hands, her touch sensual. Slowly, she moved her hands up and down, making me harder, and tearing a guttural moan from my lips.

I didn't move, enjoying her exploration of my body and

did as she pleased. When her lips touched the tip of the head, I gripped the bedsheets. Her warm, wet mouth covered as much as she could. She squeezed as she lifted her head and just as she reached the tip she went down again, filling her mouth once more. She continued moving slowly up and down my steel member, teasingly delicious. Her heated tongue flicked the crown and I struggled to contain myself. If she continued moving at that pace I'd come right then.

It was too much sensation; the work of her hands and the feel of her scorching touch sent my blood boiling. I pulled her off before I finished, and I couldn't finish— not yet.

"Your turn," I said, flipping her on her back.

She yelped as she fell against the pillows and giggled.

I stared up at her before continuing my luscious attack on her glorious body. I licked a nipple, brought the bud between my teeth and bit down hard. She gasped, then covered her mouth and leaned back into the pillows. I took that as a sign to continue.

I took my time teasing, nipping, licking and kissing my way down her body. The contours of her curves kept me pressed hard against her flesh. Her body ripe and waiting for my pleasure.

She watched with hooded eyes.

I heard her racing pulse, waiting anxiously for what was about to come next.

I teased her hard nipples and continued working down her body to the apex of her thighs. Slowly I parted her legs, glanced up at her, waiting for permission. She nodded, dropped her hands onto my head and pressed me down. I grinned.

My tongue parted her soft delicate folds; she whimpered

and writhed in response. I licked and sucked as I tasted her; a little musky, and sweet as nectar. I held onto her hips to keep her in place as my tongue danced inside her heat, then teased the sensitive nub as it eagerly ached for me.

Slowly, inserting one finger, she gasped, then two fingers. She bucked as I teased her with my fingers and tongue. She moaned profanities as she squeezed around my fingers, pleading for release.

I growled as her taste changed along with her musky scent. My growl left small vibrations against her pussy that sent her over the edge.

Slowly, I pulled out my fingers when she writhed beneath me. Then I moved above her like I was doing pushups. Waiting.

When she finally opened her passion-filled eyes, I leaned down and kissed her so she could taste herself. Her hands reached for my shoulders and pulled me closer.

"Are you ready for me?" I growled in the nape of her neck and felt her nod.

"Gods, yes," she finally said after a hard swallow.

She opened her legs wider. I grabbed my cock, pressing the tip near her opening and eased inside. She moaned as I slowly pumped into her, long deep strokes so she could get used to me. With each stroke, my flesh met hers. I bared emerging fangs when the growing need to bite her soft, delicate flesh smashed into me. I slowed my strokes, pushing down that need. I didn't know if she wanted to be my mate now or if she even knew about it. I wanted to claim every inch of her with every powerful thrust. The need to claim her as my mate consumed me when I found the pulse in her neck again. Just one bite and she would be mine forever. But she had to want this, want me.

"Kai?" She broke my train of thought, as if sensing what I yearned to do.

"I want you to be mine, but you must want it as much as me," I said through a guttural moan, sharp teeth and a rising need. I knew my green eyes burned brighter when I felt like this.

My strokes were slower yet constant, maintaining that teasing rhythm. She squeezed around me, but not enough to push her over the edge.

"I want you, Kai. Please. Make me… yours," she said frustratingly.

I sensed her hesitation. I couldn't do it. Not now. I blinked, pushing the need of flesh away. She had to be sure. Right now, she only wanted my body; to scratch a growing need. And as much as I wanted her to be mine forever, I would savor this moment with her now. We could discuss becoming mates another time.

I growled as my hips jerked, my thrusts becoming frantic and uncoordinated. She moaned as my cock throbbed and pulsed. She squeezed her orgasm around me and I pumped my heated seed into her, allowing the last few rough thrusts that sent her thighs trembling and her body shaking.

I stilled inside her, buried deep, not wanting to move away from her heat just yet. With my head near her neck, I breathed hard against her skin, sending a cascade of goose-flesh down her body.

Slowly she opened her eyes and met mine; watching with bated breath.

She moved her head to the side, waiting for my bite.

I kissed her neck instead and eased out of her, falling on my back beside her.

She trembled from the sudden loss and curled onto her side facing me.

"Why didn't you bite me? That is what must happen, isn't it? To seal the bond, so we can become one," she asked naively.

I faced her and nodded. "You know about shifter bonding?" I sounded as surprised as I felt. I hadn't mentioned the ritual to her for fear of scaring her off, and doubted she wanted to hear about the bonding that lasted a lifetime when we just met.

She nodded. "My mom spoke of it when I was a little girl. You'll need some of my blood." She swallowed hard. "And even though a bite would normally turn a human into that were-animal, during the mating ritual it would bond us. I would become a leopard metaphysically but I wouldn't change into one. I would stay human but bonded to you for life. I'd forgotten about it until I met you," she said, sounding dreamlike.

"That's right, just a small taste," I grinned predatorily. "But, you hesitated. I want you to be sure because once we do it, it's forever." I brushed hair out of her face.

She nodded and squeezed her eyes shut. "I'm afraid."

"Sacha?"

"I know I shouldn't work at the club and need to move out of his house. But…" — she shrugged, — "he will disown me, maybe hurt me. Or worse, he'll hurt you. I can't have him hurt you."

My heart warmed at her words trying to protect me, but she needed protecting.

"You're all that I want, Naomi," I said seriously. I needed her to hear what was going on inside my mind. I wanted her—no matter what. "I'm here for you. I'm your new family if you want. And, we'll have each other. And if he comes for me, I have the leap, my brothers and sisters will help us; that's what *my* family does to protect each other."

Her eyes held a sadness I didn't understand even though her lips curved at the sides. "I want to be yours, but, I need to speak to him first. Maybe he will change his mind—"

"We can do it together—"

"No, I can't risk you getting hurt."

"It will take a lot to hurt me," I smirked. "I'm hard to kill." I winked wickedly.

We fell into a comfortable silence.

She seemed content to be in my arms. And if I didn't know any better, she was resigning herself to the idea of staying with me from tonight onwards.

Naomi snuggled closer leaning her head on my shoulder, a leg over mine and her arm across my chest. "Are you purring?"

I chuckled. "Oh yes, baby, get used to it." I kissed the top of her head and held her closer. "Because you are going to hear it often."

Chapter Sixteen

NAOMI

The sound and constant vibration of Kai's purring lulled me to sleep. When I awoke alone in his bed, I hadn't felt so relaxed in years.

I stretched my limbs and sat up. I glanced around his room which was neat. Against one wall to the left stood a free-standing closet, a table and chair across from the bed, with an open laptop on the table. Beside the table was a two-seater couch. The room was small but cozy.

I fished for a clean shirt from his free-standing closet and pulled it on; I breathed in the material and smiled, it smelled like him.

Slowly, I opened the door to a man walking toward the bathroom with nothing on besides the towel over his shoulder.

He stopped, glanced over his shoulder and smiled. "Welcome, darling. If you're looking for Kai, he is that way." The man pointed in the opposite direction.

"Thank you."

"My name is Jude." He turned and proffered his hand.

He was tall with a swimmer's build, blue eyes, blond hair and boyish good looks. When he'd turned around, I caught sight of the front of him and glanced up nervously.

He chuckled. "Right, don't be shy. You'll see a lot of this around here if you intend on staying." Jude pointed to his middle, then wrapped his towel around his lower half.

I turned to him, cheeks heated, and shook his hand. Before pulling my hand free, he brought my hand to his mouth and kissed my knuckles. It seemed shifters had manners, Kai did that as well.

"How very charming," he drawled, turned on his heels and headed toward the bathroom.

"Yeah, sorry about that. Unfortunately, Jude doesn't have any tact," Kai said as he ran toward me with a bright face and smiling green eyes.

"Don't worry about it. I guess I just have to get used to it."

My words seemed to bring a low rumbling purr from Kai, and I wrapped my arms around his waist, pressing my ear against his chest.

"I like you in my shirt, by the way," he said, taking my hand and leading me down the corridor. "Let me show you around."

We walked to the end of a long corridor. Kai opened a door to another larger room filled with items.

My jaw slackened as we entered the vast room. "Wow!"

"Yeah, tell me about it. It's why there are four of us here. We watch over the Master Vampire of Sterling Meadow's most priceless artifacts."

"Léon?"

"Yes, Léon."

"How long have you worked for him?"

"Since I got here; so many years ago, I don't remember

the exact date. So far, he's been very generous and pleasant to work for, but I've seen what he can do if you cross him. People mistake his kindness for weakness and end up gone. If you understand my meaning?"

I nodded. "This must've taken him years to collect." I ran my fingers across a sarcophagus. "But then again, he's been around for centuries." I might not know much about shifters, but I knew enough about the vampires in this town.

"Yep. Back there are items he keeps in a safe and locks the entire room. I have no idea what he keeps there, just that it's incredibly rare. And back there are his cars. Come, this section is where we live with a communal kitchen and bathroom. Unfortunately, there're no ladies, but the guys won't enter if you need the bathroom."

"I'm sure it will be just fine," I said, following Kai back to their living quarters.

I couldn't explain it, only felt it; a sense of belonging with Kai. Living under Sacha's hardened hand had never felt like this; everybody was at arm's length either to protect myself or Sacha from heart ache.

As we traversed the hallway, it became brighter as the natural sunlight streamed through. I was used to hard, cold gray walls and sterile furniture; I can't remember being happy under Sacha's roof after Mom's death.

I smiled up at Kai, even though he couldn't see me, and squeezed his hand. He glanced over his shoulder, pulled me into his side for a hug and kissed my temple. I wrapped my arms around his waist and nestled into his side.

"I'm glad you brought me here last night. I like where you live."

"You do?" he sounded surprised.

"Yes," I said, nodding without looking at him. "I like it very much."

We entered the kitchen, bright orange and yellow sun rays streamed in through the little windows and warmed my bones. My arms pebbled as Kai headed for the counter leaving me near the table. Even though the kitchen was messy it was welcoming. It was lived in by people who cared for each other. I smiled to myself watching Kai move about.

"Coffee?"

"Please, with cream, no sugar."

"Hey," another man said, entering the kitchen. His jet-black hair framed green eyes, he had a square jaw with a short beard. He was taller than the others and powerfully built.

When I glanced up at him as he entered, he winked darkly.

"New toy?" he asked, sitting across from me.

Kai swatted his head, "Be respectful, this is Naomi."

"Ah, please forgive me. I thought you were Jude's plaything."

"Naomi, this is Flynn, Flynn Naomi."

He shook my hand loosely, as if afraid I was the one with sharp teeth.

I smiled but it didn't reach my eyes, wondering how many women stayed over if he thought I was *Judes's*.

As if reading my thoughts, Kai added. "I've brought no one over. Jude does, but we've asked him to stop for security reasons—"

"Let's hope Naomi isn't one who needs a souvenir."

"She won't steal. If you're going to be rude, you can make your own coffee."

"Fine." Flynn raised his hands. "I'll make my own. Just if we can't bring anyone back here then neither should you."

"This is different." Kai handed me a cup of coffee and

stepped closer to Flynn. His chest rose and fell, and a low growl escaped his lips.

"Easy leopard, I'm just pointing out the rules."

"She's my mate."

Flynn's eyes widened, and he pushed back his chair so he could stand. His eyes flitted between Kai and me. "Well, shit. You don't say. Have you completed the bonding yet? I sense nothing."

"No, not yet. Naomi wants to speak with her father first."

"Who's her father?"

"He—"

"Is Russian and very strict." I interjected. "I need a word with him before Kai and I do anything."

"I see. Well, if I were you, go with her and a couple of your leopard buddies. You know, just in case. 'Cause if he is as strict as I'm guessing, then all hell will break loose." Flynn pushed past Kai and poured himself a mug of coffee. "Just don't tell him where you work. I understand the Russian's aren't too happy with Léon."

"Why?"

"One tough Russian cheated at a card game, that *didn't take place*," — he winked while making air quotes around "didn't take place". — "They have forbidden vampires from playing card games, but that doesn't mean they don't play in secret. And now no Russian may interact with any vampire, particularly from Léon's kiss. And I heard another Russian group had moved into our town. Just prepare yourself for a whirlwind of a shit storm."

Flynn proceeded toward the door, then stopped and considered them. "Welcome, by the way. If you're serious about my boy, I wish you both the best of luck. But if you break his heart, a few of us will hurt you." He warned and exited before giving me a chance to respond.

"That was intense." I sipped my coffee, wondering who the other Russian group was. I needed to tell my father.

"Yeah, sorry about that. He has no filter. But it's what we do, we protect each other."

"I like it," I smiled and reached for Kai's hand. "I don't want to wait. I want to see my dad today. I need to know where he stands so we can move forward."

Kai nodded.

The others wouldn't understand our fast love, but I couldn't and wouldn't deny myself happiness or to love the person I wanted. And I refused to become someone's wife because of a *business deal*—a deal that wasn't mine to begin with.

I would tell my father what I wanted. I refused to sit back and have him dictate to me. Not anymore. It was my life and would live it how I wanted to.

The electricity between us was real. It was as real as the room we sat in; as real as the blood coursing through my veins and into my heart. My heart that thundered every time he touched me, kissed me, and last night was something I hadn't experienced before. My core tightened thinking about it.

As I thought about hearts, pulses racing and touching. It reminded me of a story Mom had told me; *"I believe in love at first sight. If it's the right man, you will feel it here,"* — Mom had touched my small chest, — *"and you will know. When that time comes, do everything in your power to hold on to him. He will feel it too and he will protect you."*

I blinked back the memory as I stared at Kai, drinking his coffee. We sat in comfortable silence and held hands. My eyes cast down where our fingers laced together and another surge of electricity shot up my arm. Kai turned to meet my eyes; he'd felt it too and smiled.

"Do you feel it?"

I nodded, blinking away another tear. "I don't know why, but I do. It's weird."

Kai leaned over, cupped my face and pulled me in for a kiss. His tongue needing entrance; I parted my lips and closed my eyes as his warmth caressed my skin and spread within, burning our need to touch each other. I wanted to strip him out of his shorts while he explored under my shirt when someone cleared their throat.

"Sorry to interrupt the show," Lee chuckled and entered the kitchen. "But I really need coffee." He poured his coffee as Kai sat back but kept his hand on my naked thigh, his fingers between my legs.

"Dude, you need a bell."

"You have a room."

"We actually need to go." I glanced at the clock. "I want to do this now," I said, standing and finished the last of my coffee. I placed the mug in the sink. "I want to start the rest of my life, and the sooner we do this the better."

Lee's eyes flitted from one to the other with a surprised expression. "Your father?"

I nodded.

"Well, then. You'll need backup."

Chapter Seventeen

KAI

I watched Naomi cross the street wearing a pair of my jeans that hung loosely but managed to stay on her hips with a belt, and my smallest T-shirt with the hem knotted to one side. The clothing was obviously too big for her but she made it work somehow. My body stirred remembering how she had helped herself to my things and I loved that she felt comfortable enough to do that.

She entered a house she shared with Sacha; a cozy Craftsman Bungalow. It was not the type of residence I associated with a Russian club owner who enjoyed breaking knee caps and skulls for fun. It was a family home, one I saw myself sharing with Naomi.

Naomi wanted to speak with her dad in private before introducing him to me. She wanted to explain everything and offer an ultimatum; either he accepted me, or she'd leave, never to be seen again. If there was any trouble, she'd send me a signal.

Being a shifter I could hear their conversation, but

wouldn't intrude on their privacy. If Naomi needed me, all she had to do was call for me and we would rush inside. But for now, Lee and I would sit in his Camaro and wait.

After fifteen minutes a dark SUV pulled up in front of the Camaro. Four bulky men wearing black with machine guns in their strong arms climbed out and approached the car.

"Christ, I guess they know we're here," Lee said, raising his hands.

"Yep." Slowly I raised my hands when the guns they carried pointed at our heads.

The man closest to me said, "Slowly, with your left hand, open your car door."

"Okay, just take your finger off the trigger, please. Any sudden movement and you will sprinkle those bullets all over the neighborhood."

"Move it," he growled.

"All right, all right, don't get your panties in a bunch."

"Now's not the time to provoke them, Kai," Lee said nervously.

"Yeah, yeah." I did as requested and reached for the door handle with his left hand, pushing it open with my foot.

"Get out."

The moment I climbed out of the car the tall man with the balaclava forcefully gripped my neck and led me toward the house. For a human, he was strong holding my neck like a vise grip. I sniffed, not smelling any animal scent on him apart from sweat and aftershave. He was just a block of muscle who knew how to hurt.

"Your friend can stay there," the man barked, his voice muffled through the material of his mask.

"I don't mean any harm, at least allow me to walk upright," I moaned as I was forced into a crouch position.

The brute ignored me, and continued his firm hold on my neck, keeping me hunched over like Igor until the front door. The door opened as we climbed the only step and a burly man with silver hair stood in the doorjamb. The flash of his silver eye caught my attention.

"Is dis him?"

"Yes, Sacha."

"You can let go."

The brute did as instructed and released his hold on me. I rubbed my neck and stood tall, trying my best to glower at the man, but he was a whole head taller and paid me no attention.

"You're da waste of flesh with his hooks in my Naomi?"

I didn't know if the man in black would shoot if I responded, so thought it best to remain quiet until Sacha asked an actual question.

"Come in." Sacha stepped to one side, allowing me access. "Do anything and I'll have Demetri blow your head off. We have good bullets in guns that kill shifters." He patted his gun.

"I don't want to cause any trouble, sir," I said, raising both hands.

"Too late! You've already done so," Sacha said, closing the door behind me. "Go there." He pointed toward a room on my right.

I entered the living area and found Naomi on the couch with her face in her hands, quietly sobbing.

"This is for Michail."

A blast sounded. Pain laced my shoulder and I flew into the wall. The impact was sudden. My back ached as a warm liquid oozed down my back. I saw darkness at first then slowly my vision returned along with a splitting headache. With a groan, I sat up and leaned on my right elbow.

When I focused on Sacha, anger filled my veins at the man who'd shot me and silently vowed to kill him.

Chapter Eighteen

NAOMI

"No!" I jumped to my feet and stood in front of Kai protecting him. "You'll have to go through me to get to him—"

"No, I can handle it."

"Not when he shoots your head off."

"Get out of the way, Naomi," Sacha said, motioning with the gun for me to move out of his way. "This ends now. Besides, I want to turn him into a rug after he shifts."

I shook my head. "I'd rather die than stay with you or marry someone I don't love. If Mom was here, she wouldn't allow the marriage. And she'd want us to be together." I touched Kai's shoulder. "I love him, Papa. Why can't you see that and allow us to be together?"

It was only once the word left my mouth, did I register that I said the l-word. But Sacha needed to know how we felt about each other.

I loved Kai, but didn't know if he loved me back. But now wasn't the time to dissect my feelings but to get Kai safely out of there before Sacha shot him again.

"You just met the fool." Sacha shook his head. "You are a disgrace, Naomi. You are no daughter of mine. You be with him, you are not welcome here." His voice broke toward the end of the sentence and lowered his weapon.

His words hurt. He was my only family. I did my best to stop the tears from flowing down my cheeks.

When I felt brave enough, I exhaled a shaky breath and lifted my chin. If this was what he wanted, then so be it. I tried to reason with him; I explained everything in our private conversation but he wasn't listening. He didn't want to hear.

I felt the cold of his heart for years after my mother's death. If I left today, it would be no different. I was closer to my mother, anyway. And I had Kai; our feelings for each other were real.

"If that's what you want—"

"It is. You have five minutes to get him out before I kill you both." Sacha left the room.

Silence pierced my ears, and I refused to cry again; not for a father who only cared about business, or for a loveless marriage to a man who would only see me as a possession; especially if he was anything like his father.

I wanted to make peace with my father and he responded by shooting Kai. I didn't have a chance to tell him about the other Russians in town but he would soon find out.

I turned to find Kai leaning against the wall with a pool of blood beneath him.

"You need help." I pulled on his good arm to help him stand.

"We have a doctor we use, we can call on the way to the Leap."

Chapter Nineteen

NAOMI

The men in balaclavas, black cargo pants and black tactical vests stepped to one side as Lee helped me carry Kai to the car. Once Kai was in the front, I climbed into the backseat, locking him in place with the seat belt and wrapped my arms around his chest. I pressed my cheek against his head and whimpered.

Kai patted my arm and nudged my cheek. "Hey, we will try again. Your father will come around."

"It's not that. I thought I lost you." I gripped his shoulders as Lee pulled away from the curb and smashed the gas.

"Ah, babe," Kai said, reaching for my head and pulling me closer. "I'll be okay. I don't want to freak you out, but after Mel removes the bullet and assess me, I'll shift into my leopard. I will need to eat then rest. If you need anything Lee will look after you while I'm down."

I shook my head. "No, I don't want to leave you."

"Shh, it will be all right. You'll see." Kai closed his eyes for only a second.

Chapter Twenty

NAOMI

"Kai?" I shrieked, frantically nudging Kai to wake up, but it didn't help. "Lee, what's going on? Is he supposed to be like this?"

Lee seemed nervous as he glanced at Kai and shook his head. He tried to keep the car on the road and narrowly missed a couple in their car. "No, we don't sleep after a bullet enters us."

"Sacha said it was strong bullets, but I don't know what he means."

"Shit! Okay, don't panic. We are five minutes away from the Leap. I need you to keep watch and let me know if he stops breathing."

"What? Is he going to be okay?" I carefully kept hold of Kai's head to monitor his breathing with my legs bent on the back seat. I didn't care if my shoes scratched the leather seats, Kai's wellbeing came first.

"I don't know if it's the same bullets we've been hearing about, but Mel should be able to help him."

"Should?" I asked with panic laced in that one word.

Before Lee answered he swerved, cutting in front of another car who leaned on the horn and pointed fingers. Lee ignored the other driver as he concentrated on speeding down the winding road. He skipped a Stop sign, cut a corner as he rode over a mailbox and hit the accelerator.

The road we travelled stretched for a distance with fewer houses and more forest on either side. This was a section of Sterling Meadow I'd never travelled before. Sacha had me driven everywhere and I was never allowed to venture anywhere alone.

It still amazed me how I was able to go to the book shop by myself. When I thought about it, I wasn't really by myself —I was still followed.

I shook off the thoughts; my father was no longer in my life and now I might lose Kai, too. My chest ached as I clung to him, pressing my hand near his heart; its beat was steady but slow. I bit my lip as tears flowed. I couldn't lose him too. I had to have faith. This Mel person would save Kai, he would shift and everything would be okay. I had to have strength to get through this.

As Lee drove maniacally to our destination, my hand on Kai's chest, I marveled at the passing tall trees. The smell of pines assaulted my olfactory senses and took me to a forgotten memory. I closed my eyes and held onto Kai.

When the vehicle came to an abrupt stop, my eyes fluttered open. We parked near a large house on the side of the road with the forest as its backyard. It was beautiful.

I kissed Kai's cheek. "We're here, babe," I whispered, assuming it was the leap; remembering Kai had said it sat on the edge of the forest.

Lee jumped out and opened the passenger's side door and lifted Kai over his shoulder as if he weighed nothing. "Follow me," he said as he jogged to the front door.

The door opened, and a woman greeted Lee.

"You must be Naomi." The woman took my hand in her smaller one and led me to the room Lee had disappeared into. "My name is Anne, the former leader of the leap," she smiled sweetly, but I caught the worry in her brown/green eyes. Her silver hair cut short, pixie style, with fine lines near her eyes and mouth. She was motherly as she continued holding my hand. I was grateful for the comfort.

"What happened?" I flinched at the man's deep, commanding voice, watching him traversed down the corridor. His blond hair shaved at the sides and long on top, framing grass green eyes.

I stared at his heavenly features and caught a golden light pass through his eyes. My arms pebbled at his presence and confusion set in.

An uneasiness settled in my bones and glanced at Kai, who was on the bed, still unconscious with blood everywhere. He was losing too much blood, but there was something else. I felt his pain and him slowly slipping away.

Blood drained from my face as Anne struggled to keep me on my feet.

"Help me Sebastian, I think this one is about to crash."

In one swift motion I was in the air, my ears buzzed followed by tunneling vision until the darkness swallowed me whole.

Chapter Twenty-One

NAOMI

I stood alone in a forest, staring up at the sun as it beat against my skin. The air smelled of honey and rain.

Someone coughed.

I turned and headed in their direction, coming to a stop when I saw Kai resting against a fallen tree. Panic set in and I ran toward him, skidding to a stop. I fell beside him and sucked in a frantic breath. Carefully, I cupped his face, his skin cold and pale.

"Don't leave me," I whispered, tears marking my cheeks. I leaned over and kissed his cool lips.

"Wait for me, I'll see you soon," Kai managed to say through dry lips. "It means the world to me that you're here with me."

"I don't understand?" I asked, surveying our surroundings. "It's just a forest."

"It's the Leap. And you are here, with me, with my leopard."

"How can that be?"

Before Kai responded, his heart thumped beneath my hand, my body floated away.

My eyes flitted open, jackknifing out of the bed, almost crashing to the ground. My head ached, but my chest hurt more.

Glancing around the unknown room, I couldn't remember what had happened, but knew something terrible had gone wrong.

The smell of pines and the green forest flashed before me, and the sensation of the warm sun on my skin.

Kai.

With a hand over my heart, I remembered...

I darted for the door, yanked it open and left it to smash loudly against the wall. Not knowing where I was, I tried the room next door.

My chest rising and falling when I saw him. He seemed so helpless lying on the bed with a sheet covering him from his waist down. They had bandaged his left shoulder and chest, with a blue solution going into his hand via an IV drip. He lay still, eyes closed, and my heart dropped to my toes. I couldn't tell if he was breathing. And he hadn't shifted into his leopard.

"He's resting," a woman said behind me.

I recoiled and turned around; a woman stared with big brown eyes, platinum hair that reached her shoulders, and a sad smile.

"Is he breathing?"

She nodded. "Uh-huh."

"He said he needed to shift. Why hasn't he shifted?"

"It's going to be okay, Naomi." The woman placed a

calming hand on my elbow and I relaxed. "My name is Mel—"

"The doctor?"

Mel nodded. "Yes, I'm the doctor to all the were-animals," she said, keeping her hand on my elbow. "I won't lie to you, Naomi, but there was a complication," she said gravely. "The bullet I extracted from his shoulder stopped him from shifting. It was the type of ammo they only sell on the black market. It's new and it's nasty, but you got here in time and I could remove all the fragments without it shattering and entering his bloodstream. The blue solution is something we made ourselves in case one of our own got shot with these bullets. It's filled with epinephrine to speed up the recovery and to wake him. When that happens, he'll be able to shift and heal. I've only used it once before but it's potent."

"But he'll be okay?" I asked, chewing my lip when panic spiked again.

Mel squeezed my elbow. "He is going to be okay. You can sit with him if you like?"

"I would, yes."

Mel let go and I furrowed my brows. "That was weird. Was it you? I don't know how to explain it, but your touch—"

"I can calm others, yes. It's my secret weapon." Mel winked. "Let me know if you need my help again," she added and disappeared down the corridor.

I closed the door behind me and approached Kai. He hadn't moved since I first entered his room. When I touched his hand, he didn't move, and he was hot. The blue solution made his veins blue as it traveled throughout his body; reminding me of roads on a map. I cupped his face and neared, my lips touched his ever so delicately, afraid to hurt him.

"Come back to me," I whispered near his ear with my cheek against his.

There was no response. Needing to be closer, I climbed onto the bed beside him and snuggled into his arms.

His body was hot against mine but I didn't care if I overheated, this was where I wanted to be.

Chapter Twenty-Two

KAI

Heat sear through my veins and I wanted to tear my skin off. My body ached and my chest weighed down with unrelenting tightness.

Memories flashed before me, remembering Sacha and being shot in the back. *Who did that?* A coward. And the bullets he had used told me the type of man Sacha really was—a cold-blooded killer.

The bed moved, and my eyes shot open. The weight on my chest shifted and hair tickled my nose. Her smell awoke beast and I smiled as thoughts of her came into view; her body, her smile, and her scent. I moved my arms, enveloping her, and held her tighter.

"Kai?" Naomi moved away and sat up. She reached for my face, I moaned, she apologized and kissed gently. "How are you feeling?"

"Better with you in my arms." I motioned for her to lay with me. "How long have I been asleep?"

"A few hours. I'm not sure. I passed out when they brought you here," she smiled sheepishly.

"Are you okay?"

"I am now."

"Help me up."

Naomi climbed off the bed and helped me to sit. She fixed the pillows behind me, but I didn't want to lie down.

"I need to shift. Once that happens, I'll heal quicker and it won't leave a scar," I said, feeling the bandage and plaster over the wound.

"Okay." She nodded and stood back, giving him space.

I ripped the needle out of my hand and shuddered. "At least Mel's concoction worked," I grinned, rounding my shoulders and stood tall; at least a head taller than Naomi now that she was barefoot. The sheet fell away from my naked body. Naomi swallowed hard.

"You can have this soon, baby girl. Let me heal and you can have your way with me," I grinned, watching her blush.

I crooked a finger. She neared. I cupped her face, and she wrapped her cool hands around my waist. Crushing my lips against hers, I wanted more, but had to tear myself away.

"Stand back." I nudged her away. "And remember, I won't hurt you, but it could be scary the first time you see the change."

I kissed her chastely one last time and motioned for her to stand farther back. Beast rippled beneath my skin, eager to explode out of my body and heal. I growled low as my joints popped; the pain seared through my shoulder, making me want to shift quicker.

I ripped the plaster and bandage off my chest, the hole stitched but continued bleeding. I wasn't worried, my body would heal.

My limbs stretched and pulled as fur flowed over my

body. Falling onto all fours, I arched my back as beast pushed to the surface with a roar.

Footsteps neared, followed by yelling.

I shifted to my spotted leopard as Lee entered the room.

Chapter Twenty-Three

NAOMI

I jumped onto the bed the moment Kai exploded into his leopard; his fur soft and thick, and golden with dark spots grouped in rosettes. He made a low rasping cough sound as he stretched his limber body.

I'd never seen a leopard up close before, but knew they weren't as big as Kai; they were small in comparison to Kai's larger, bulkier form. His muscles rippled beneath the skin as he turned around and stalked the bed.

I swallowed hard but dared not move; worried if I made any sudden movements he'd pounce.

"It's all right, he won't hurt you. He's been a cheeky leopard for many years and can control his beast. He's just showing off now," Lee said, leaning against the doorjamb.

Kai placed his front paws on the bed and spoke. His baritone pitch came out hoarse and raspy. "Naomi, love."

My heart swelled with love, and forgot all fear. It was only Kai. He'd never hurt me. I leaned forward and placed my hand under his enormous jaw, tickling him, then scratched behind his ear and he purred.

"All right, big kitty." Lee tugged on Kai's shoulders. "Are you hungry?"

Kai roared.

"Is it difficult to speak when like that."

"It can be," Lee offered. "We can get one or two words out and hope the person understands us. But we rarely need to speak. Our calls and roars are understood by our kind." He proffered his hand to help me off the bed. "You will get used to it. Walk with me while I get our bad boy here to the cages."

"Are you caging him?"

"No, we're just going to get him fed and then he'll sleep it off while he heals."

"Oh."

I followed Lee and Kai down the flight of stairs toward the basement with four cages. It smelled like a petting zoo. In each cage was some hay with a large bowl of water. The far side held an enclosure with five goats.

"Which one do you want?" Lee asked.

Kai roared as he lifted his head and eyed the goat in the far corner.

"Yeah, he smells good, doesn't he?" Lee grabbed the black goat with the alien horizontal rectangular pupil. It screamed as Lee pulled it to the cage where Kai waited.

I didn't want to watch Kai rip the goat apart, but knew I had to. To be with Kai, I needed to learn everything about his world. And as unpleasant as it was, I had to see it all and that included seeing him attack and eat a goat.

I also had to make peace with my new life and forget the old one; including Sacha. It shocked me how he shot Kai without blinking; he was a heartless monster and I wanted nothing to do with him. My heart ached but would get used to it.

My stomach twisted and turned watching Kai bite the goats throat until it died, then he pulled apart the goat's legs. At least he killed it as humanely as possible. It was food for their kind, and he needed to eat to heal. It was a necessity, not a sport

I waited in silence, never turning away.

Lee stood beside me and waited patiently; it was as if he understood my need to stay with Kai. And I was grateful for the company.

Lee had left the cage closed but unlocked. When Kai finished his meal, he lay down and closed his eyes. As he rested, I watched in awe how the wound knitted together and healed. It was a mystery and miracle. And I witnessed him becoming whole again.

My eyes misted, not understanding my emotions. Perhaps I was in mourning over my father disowning me and blaming me for everything that went wrong in his life—including Mom's death. That I was unwelcome in his home, and to him I was dead.

Then the stress of Kai getting shot and the thought of losing him was overwhelming. I doubted whether I would survive the loss of him, too.

As I watched my mate rest, my chest filled with hope. He was going to be okay. And we had a chance to be together. That in such a short time we'd gone through so much and I knew that I loved him.

I was happy to be his and couldn't wait to be bound to him.

Chapter Twenty-Four

KAI

I hugged Anne and thanked her for everything.

Mel had stayed the whole day to ensure I was fine and I hugged her too.

"Don't get shot," Mel teased as she exited. "And look after Naomi, she seems like a frightened little bird."

"Yeah," I said, glancing over my shoulder at Anne whispering to Naomi—I shuddered at what they were discussing and grateful Anne didn't have any baby pictures of me. To the Leap, Anne was the leader everyone had grown to love as a mother. "Her father hasn't exactly been a role model, and her mom died when she was young."

"She has you, and now she has the Leap. That's all that counts."

I hugged Mel again, grateful for her service to all shifters. The Leap would suffer if she no longer helped. She was a were-wolf and rare soul who came into everybody's lives when it counted the most.

As I closed the front door, large hands gripped my neck. I thought of Sacha's men, especially the one who had grabbed me, and I moved on instinct. I hit the man in the ribs followed by a cracking sound. Sebastian coughed and let go.

"Shit, sorry, Sebastian. You gave me a fright."

"It's okay, I should've realized." He slapped my back. "How are you feeling?" Sebastian winced and rubbed his side.

After I shifted into my leopard, I ate, napped, and shifted back into my human form, all within eight hours, which was a record. Usually I slept the night before changing back. Whatever was in the blue solution had sped up the healing process and gave me enough energy to shift so soon.

"I feel good." Kai turned to see Naomi, who smiled at Anne, stole a glance my way and continued with her conversation.

"I hear you two are fated?"

Heat stirred within just thinking about Naomi becoming mine. "Yeah, can you believe it? I almost lost hope. I thought Lee and I would keep each other company for the rest of our lives. Can you imagine, I think we'd kill each other. Luckily, all that changed when I saw her." I glanced at Sebastian and with a serious tone, asked. "Did you experience the same with Blaire?"

Sebastian fell quiet for a moment, then finally said, "When I picked her up in that cold alley, I felt something. At first, it was hard to make out what it was because of that black poison coursing through her veins. But then as she healed, we got to know each other pretty well. I think because I'm a hybrid it's different for me yet similar. I didn't get that immediate zing like you two have." One side of his mouth curved upward as he considered Naomi.

I nodded, understanding what he meant. Sebastian was

half-vampire, half-leopard; he had the best of both worlds and extremely powerful. His brother, Léon, was Master Vampire of Sterling Meadow and my boss. Léon and Sebastian were rightful leaders of their respective groups and stood together to make our City great.

"Yeah, it feels as though she struck me," I said. Then my thoughts drifted to Sacha who had used special ammunition to kill me. I wondered about the course of action against him, and the new Russian group everyone was speaking about.

"Did you find out who the supplier is for the ammo?" I asked, rubbing the wound that was no longer there.

"We're still trying to figure out who brought those here and have a meeting with the WAA later today."

The WAA was the Were-Animal Alliance, headed by Sebastian and a handful of the leaders from the other were-animal groups; lions, rats, wolves, and even tigers.

"Can you ask around about Sacha, and the other Russian group. I doubt Naomi can give us more information than what we already have."

Sebastian nodded. "If they don't want shifters at their club, then they've come to the wrong town. When I meet the leaders later, we'll discuss what to do with them. They can't stay here and behave that way. We don't discriminate."

"Good, and I'm sure Léon would get involved if he needed to."

Sebastian grinned. "Yeah, I'm sure the Russians would love that." He squeezed my shoulder. "I'm running late. I'll see you at the full moon harvest if not before then."

Much was happening and I hoped nobody else got hurt by those bullets. They were nasty.

Chapter Twenty-Five

KAI

It was two days before the full moon, and I felt the pull of the silver as beast rippled beneath my skin.

Naomi lay beside me on my bed at the warehouse. She slept peacefully for someone who had gone through so much.

A week had passed since her dad had shot me and her father had disowned her. She hadn't spoken about that day and avoided the subject whenever I brought it up.

During the week we got to know each other's bodies intimately. We spent all day and night sharing our thoughts and ideas. We showered together, washed each other, discovered what the other liked to eat. Everything.

And I loved spending all my time with her. She made me laugh, made me feel whole. And when she felt sad or lost in the shadows of her mind, I brought her back to the surface; back to me.

Some mornings she would make coffee and breakfast, then the next day it was my turn to spoil her. Our actions and affection toward each other was simple yet it meant the world. This was what was lacking in my life and she fit perfectly with me.

We lay face to face with my arm over her waist, savoring the feeling of her so close. I listened to her light breathing as she slept and stared at her, not believing my luck that she was mine.

She moved onto her side and I brought her into the curve of my body. As I breathed in so did she; and my heart beating in time with hers. It was a glorious feeling and one I'd treasure forever.

The moment shattered when Lee burst through the door. "Get up. Sacha is here," Lee said breathlessly. Sweat peppered his forehead, his brown eyes wide.

Naomi started, sat up and stared with matching expression. "Oh, no. How did he know I was here?"

"He's probably always known. Come." I pulled on pants and handed her a clean shirt.

I held onto Naomi trying to warm her body. She shivered even though it wasn't cold inside the warehouse.

"Is he alone?"

"From what I could see, yes," Lee said, walking ahead of us.

When we reached the security door, we scanned the monitors and flicked through the channels to review the live footage.

Sacha leaned against his vintage Jaguar, his meaty arms folded across his broad chest. He wore jeans with a black T-shirt and sneakers. It was a strange sight to see a man who he'd only seen wearing dark tailored suits.

"He never wears jeans," Naomi said, staring at the monitor. She confirmed my suspicions.

"Does anything feel off to you? I need to know before I open the door," I asked, my tone serious.

Nervously, Naomi glanced at the monitor, then back at me. "I don't know. But it's strange he's in jeans and sneakers. And he's driving his favorite car. He never takes it out of the garage."

"Okay, I don't see anyone else with him, but prepare for the worst. And stay out of sight until I tell you," I said sternly, slowly unlocking the door. I opened it; the creaking of the hinges like blades down my back.

The moment Sacha saw me, he pushed away from his car and approached.

I raised my hands to stop him. "Stay where you are. What do you want? You've made your stance perfectly clear—"

"Where's Naomi?"

I fell silent, narrowing my eyes at the large Russian. Anger filled my veins but I wouldn't attack first, even though I wanted to rip his heart out.

"You've already disowned her. Why should she see you?" I left out the part about him trying to kill me but this wasn't about me; this was about Sacha and Naomi.

"Please tell her I miss her." He choked on his words. When he caught his breath, he added, "The club isn't the same without her."

Naomi grumbled curse words only I heard, but dared not glance over my shoulder.

"She doesn't work for you anymore, Sacha. I'll ask one last time. What is your reason for coming here?" I stepped forward so the door closed. I didn't want Sacha seeing Naomi and storm the entrance.

"I was wrong. Please tell her I want to speak to her, in private."

The door flew open and Naomi exited; a flurry of emotions crossing her features. She stood beside me, slipping her smaller hand into mine. I wanted to chastise her for coming out, but she was her own person—and from her expression she was about to rip into her father.

"Whatever you have to say to me, you can say in front of Kai." Naomi wrapped her arms around my waist, I pulled her closer and kissed the top of her head.

Sacha stepped closer but kept his distance. "I wanted to protect you from them," — his eyes flitted to mine then back to Naomi, — "but no matter what I try to do to persuade you from meeting them it's clearly fated you will meet someone." His shoulders sagged, and he exhaled a ragged breath. "A shifter killed your mom. That's why I did it. To protect you."

"How do you know?" She asked, the lines between her eyes deepening.

"I was with her that day. She was seeing someone else." His watery eyes met Naomi's, even the metallic orb in its socket leaked. "I followed her. Those days shifters hid in the shadows, much like vampires. When I caught sight of her lover, it enraged me and I wanted to hurt him. But then… his wife changed into her leopard and killed your mother. I had no weapons to defend and I couldn't help her. I later learned your mother wanted her lover to change her; she wanted to leave us for *him*." He closed his eyes as the tears flowed down his cheeks. When he opened them, the one looked like shards of glass. "I can't lose you too."

"You almost killed him—"

"I'm sorry," Sacha said with raised hands. "It enraged me to see you with him. It took me back to that time with your mother."

"I love him and want to be with him. Can you understand and accept that?" Naomi asked, her tone harsh.

Sacha flexed his fists. He was restraining himself; if given the chance, he'd ram his fist down my throat to expel the pent-up frustration after so many years.

Sacha grunted his understanding but whether he accepted it was another thing.

"I must know." He stepped aside so we could see his car. "Michail isn't getting better," he said, glowering at me. "Can you help him."

"Is that why you're here? For Michail?" Naomi snapped and folded her arms.

"No, of course not. It's not the only reason I came. I wanted to see if you're okay." Sacha fell silent for a moment as he stared at Naomi, then me. "I see you are taken care of."

"She's my responsibility now," I said. "And I can help with him." I jerked my chin in Michail's direction. Sebastian was investigating the source of the ammunition, but unsuccessfully thus far. If Sacha needed help, perhaps I could use it to our advantage.

Naomi protested, but I winked so only she saw.

"I can help Michail, but in return I need something from you."

"What?" Sacha barked, clearly unhappy with the ultimatum.

"Bless our bonding and tell us who your supplier is for the ammunition you used on me."

"Never."

"Then leave." I turned and escorted Naomi toward the door.

"Wait." Sacha opened the car door and helped Michail

out. Sacha kept his arm around Michail to keep him upright.

Perspiration soaked the pale man's clothing. His eyes were yellow, and the bite on his neck was severely infected. It puzzled me; Michail didn't turn into a leopard which should have happened already. This was the first time I'd bitten a human who had lived. I knew the process intimately and Michail should be a leopard. Yet, he wasn't.

"Is this normal?" Naomi angled her head to the side as she stared at the dying man.

I shook my head, pulling my cellphone out of my pocket. I dialed Mel's number and spoke quickly, giving her a summary of what had happened and our location.

I pocketed my cellphone and turned to Sacha. "Bless our bonding and give me the info on the ammunition or I will phone Mel again and tell her to stay away."

Sacha pursed his lips.

"Wait, before you answer him, answer me. Why do you care so much about Michail? He's only an employee, yet you cradle him in your arms. When I saw how Kai had bitten him, I was sure he would die or you'd have him dumped somewhere to die alone." Naomi approached the two men. "Who is he to you?" she demanded in a low voice.

Michail lifted his head and lovingly rested it on Sacha's shoulder. Sacha pulled Michail closer to his body as he kept him standing and squeezed his waist.

"Why didn't you tell me?"

"I was afraid." Sacha's voice broke as he tried to keep up with his bravado.

Naomi pinched the bridge of her nose, and I was sure she'd shed a tear. After a moment, she glanced up.

"When he's healed, and a were-leopard, he'll need a home." She stepped in front of me, I snaked my hands around her waist and pulled her closer to my front. "I'm sure Kai and his Leap will accept him. Do you understand what I'm saying, Father?"

Sacha nodded. "Yes, I understand. Please help him. And to answer your question," — his eyes flitted to me, — "I will bless your bonding. And the man you seek is also the maker of the bullets."

Chapter Twenty-Six

KAI

Lee and I joined Sebastian at the Bullet Maker's house. We met Sacha at the front door, along with five of his bodyguards. It was overkill to have so many dangerous men, but the Bullet Maker enjoyed booby-trapping his house.

Sacha arched an eyebrow as we approached, raising his hand, but the door opened before he could strike the wood with a knuckle.

"What are you doing here?" the Bullet Maker grunted, keeping his front door ajar.

"No-one needs to get hurt, Maker. I've brought these fine gentlemen along because they have questions. And I thought it best it be a conversation instead of having your house swarmed by every single shifter in town."

The Bullet Maker snorted, that stomach turning sound as he sucked snot from the back of his throat, opened the screen door and spat on the grass. He rubbed his enormous belly, pulled down his off-white vest, but it didn't cover everything and opened the door.

"Fine, but touch nothing. I've rigged the house."

"You have my word," Sacha said, entering first, followed by Sebastian, Lee, then me.

The Maker sat on a worn couch with cigarette burns; as if he ate, drank, and slept there. The house smelled of rotten eggs, feet and sweat.

I desperately wanted to block my nose but knew if I did that I'd taste the disgusting aromas of the house.

One look in Lee's direction and knew he struggled to hold his composure too.

We remained standing while the Maker stared daggers at us.

"Enough of this," Sebastian started. "To whom do you supply the ammunition you make?"

"What's it to you?"

"I'm the leader of the leopards, and I sit on the WAA. We need to know who you supply and to stop making ammunition—"

"Or what?"

"Today will be the last day you breathe."

Sacha stepped backward, leaned against the wall and folded his arms. His metallic eye glinted sinisterly in the dim light. Today he'd worn one of his tailored navy suits; a stark contrast to his outfit from yesterday.

When Mel had arrived and had treated Michail; she'd discovered he had a rare blood type—hence the infection. She'd given him a blood transfusion to save his life, but she couldn't rid him of his animal—his change was inevitable.

At least now, Michail would heal, shift, and I had welcomed him as a leopard. Now we needed Sebastian to accept him. That's why Sacha had to join us at the Bullet Maker's house—if all went smoothly, Sebastian would accept Michail; and Sacha if he was so inclined.

The Maker snorted and shook his head while he laughed. "You're kidding, right?"

"Does it look like I'm kidding?" Sebastian said, irritated. "I don't care about you, and it looks as though nobody does either."

The Maker glanced around nervously.

"I sense you have something over there." Sebastian pointed to his right—a small, shiny black box. It stood out compared to the rest of the place. "What would happen if I picked it up?"

"Don't!" The Maker jumped to his feet to block Sebastian's path. "Don't touch it. If you do, this entire house blows up."

"Answer my questions."

The Maker's shoulders sagged. His eyes flitted from Sebastian's, to Sacha, then Lee and then me, before looking Sebastian again.

"I only supply to the Russians, Sacha and Demetri—"

"The same Demetri who works for me?" Sacha asked confusingly.

"No, the other one." The Maker averted Sacha's piercing gaze.

"What? Is Demetri Petrov here?" Sacha pushed away from the wall, sounding flabbergasted, and swore in Russian.

The Maker nodded as he stared at the scuff marks on the floor.

"Answer me, Maker?"

The Maker lifted his head. "Yes, and I've heard about your history with him."

"And you sold him the same ammunition."

"I had to…" He swallowed hard. "He has my wife."

The Maker broke down and cried. He told us about

what had happened. He'd asked Demetri Petrov to help get his family to this country, and when he did, he kept his wife as ransom, forcing the Maker to make the bullets for him. When Sacha had approached him for his order, the Maker saw it as an opportunity to have Sacha on his side. He needed Sacha's help to bring his wife home. He knew of Sacha's history with Demetri Petrov and hoped he would act in kindness.

It was then I realized Demetri was Sacha's wife's lover and had not died as Sacha had first thought. That's why he looked so surprised to hear his name.

Sacha was outside speaking with his men.

The Maker was making tea.

Sebastian, Lee, and me conversed in the living area.

It made sense; if Sacha didn't help the Maker, it was possible Demetri would kill his wife. But Demetri still needed bullets. And Sacha wanted to stop Demetri for personal reasons. But it was up to the WAA to rid the town of all the unsavories.

Chapter Twenty-Seven

KAI

Demetri crossed the street and headed toward the abandoned building.

The Maker called him with a time and address for the drop.

Shards of glass littered the floor like confetti with puddles of water left from the previous night's rain.

Demetri entered the building, almost tripping when he saw Sacha standing on a clean spot in the center of the dank room. He pulled his weapon, aiming it at the man waiting for him like the Grim Reaper.

"What are you doing here?" Demetri asked.

Sacha didn't hesitate. He may not be a shifter but he was lightning fast. He grabbed the gun out of his hands and using the momentum to knock him off his feet. They crashed to the ground with a loud thud and Demetri at the bottom.

Sacha pinned his arms to his sides with his legs and started punching him in the face, blood spraying every-where. Sacha was going to kill him with his hands.

Once Sacha was content he'd smashed Demetri's face enough times he fell off, puked one side, and nursed his split knuckles.

Slowly, Demetri sat up, spitting blood and straightened his broken nose. He pulled his fine suit jacket straight but it was badly torn.

"I thought you were dead, *old friend*." Sacha stood slowly, maintaining a suspicious eye.

"She left me for dead," Demetri said, standing and lifted my chin.

"And my wife?"

Demetri swallowed hard, and glanced around. He picked up his gun and headed toward the nearest open window.

"I wouldn't if I were you. My men have rifles trained on every opening."

Sebastian came out from behind a broken locker. Lee stood up from the drum he hid behind, while I approached from the back.

Demetri spun around the moment he heard footsteps, aiming his weapon at me, wincing in pain.

"What is the meaning of this?" he said, pointing his weapon at each of us, then spun around and pointed it at Sacha again.

"What are you doing with the ammunition?" Sacha stepped forward and pressed his forehead against the barrel of his gun, squeezing his eyes shut.

Demetri lowered his weapon. He couldn't pull the trigger; he seemed nervous as his eyes flitted between us leopards.

"Answer me!"

Demetri flinched. "I use them to threaten the shifters.

My employer demands that I recoup money from as many as possible. I've shot no one—"

"Then how come we've heard of others being injured."

"Not by me or my people."

"But it has gotten out?"

"Yes, one box was stolen. A man who no longer works for me, or breathes. I have contained it."

"You need to destroy them and send the Maker his wife."

Demetri furrowed his brows. "She wishes not to return to him. Have you seen the slob? He's disgusting. She had the choice, and she begged me not to go back. And her children are old enough to make their own decisions and prefer to live with her."

"Where is she? The Maker needs to know so he can speak with her himself."

"I've told him where they are and he has already spoken with her. I guarantee you he is long gone. He told you lies to get you out of his house."

Sacha glanced at Sebastian, who was already on the phone; I surmised to ensure the Maker was still at home.

"What about Mia, my wife?" Sacha asked again.

"Melissa attacked your wife, shot at me, then turned the gun on herself."

"She hit you in the head. I saw you fall."

"I turned my head to protect Mia, the bullet struck the side of my head, but because of the angle it exited." Demetri pointed to an area on his forehead; the entrance and exit wounds he'd sustained. He was a shifter and had healed but a scar remained as a reminder.

Demetri begged Sacha for forgiveness. He admitted to ruining their friendship by falling in love with his wife and ultimately it was his fault she had died.

Demetri explained to Sacha that after the shooting, leopards from his Leap had found him and cared for him. After he shifted and healed, he had searched for Sacha. But by then he and Naomi had already fled the country, making it difficult to explain what had happened.

Demetri told Sacha that Mia had loved him once and he didn't plan on falling in love with her. She wanted to be part of his world. She wanted to tell Sacha, to explain, but Demetri's wife had arrived at the park and had taken her anger out on Mia and Demetri, then killed herself.

Demetri hadn't forgiven himself for what had happened and that's why he'd been searching for Sacha all these years. He'd vowed to find Sacha to tell him the truth, had followed their trail across the country but hadn't had the guts to approach Sacha when he arrived in Sterling Meadow.

Sacha touched his face near his artificial eye. He explained how he had channeled his fury by fighting a gang before going home that dreadful evening; one man had a switchblade and stabbed him in the face.

The silence hung in the air as the men glared sadly at each other.

Demetri finally added the reason he asked the Maker for the bullets because of the pushback from the shifters.

Sebastian glanced my way and I shrugged; I didn't know of any leopards with gambling debts.

Demetri didn't want to join our Leap for fear we'd think he was weak. The leopards who had gambling debts thought they could get away with not paying, thinking Sebastian would help them. Meanwhile, Demetri's boss travelled back to Russia and instructed him to handle his gambling business for him.

Demetri exhaled a shaky breath and collapsed on the

cold, wet ground. I guessed his conscience was clear and could finally rest.

By early evening Sacha had arranged with Demetri's boss that he would offer the gambling service and recoup the money owed—without using excessive force. He also secured Demetri and his men under his employ.

Sacha was a potent businessman who would ensure no shifters got hurt, but only if they continued to pay with Sebastian's backing.

Chapter Twenty-Eight

NAOMI

I listened intently as Kai explained what had transpired between my father and Demetri, and what had happened to my mother all those years ago. It brought closure knowing how she had died—for love even though it had cost her her life—and it explained why my father hated shifters; particularly were-leopards.

The man known as the Bullet Maker had almost gotten away, but Sebastian's leopards had detained him before he skipped town.

I frowned when Kai explained how my father had gained more employees and now worked with another Russian boss. Which meant if I continued working for him, I worked for the new Russian boss, too.

And with the WAA's help, those shifters who owed money would pay their debts. Nobody wanted any were-animal to get hurt because they owed money.

Kai and Lee had gone back to the Maker's house and had destroyed everything used to create the ammunition.

"And now I'm hungry," Kai said with a toothy grin,

pressing his soft lips against mine and I melted against his honed body.

Kai would never be an alpha male for the Leap, nor would he be rich, but he was mine. And he would do everything he could to keep me safe and provide for me like he'd been doing the last week. And without realizing it, he had brought me and Sacha closer than we had ever been.

Kai was everything in a man I had ever dreamed of and he ticked all my boxes; trustworthy, dominant, my protector, and he oozed deliciousness I would devour.

We might not travel the world, or live in a mansion, but I saw our future in his bright green eyes. I loved the way he touched and made me feel. I was the only one in his life and knew he didn't want another. He set my soul on fire and made me feel alive.

And underneath his furry exterior was a sweet, kind, yet scary dangerous man. Just the way I wanted.

Chapter Twenty-Nine

KAI

I traced the soft skin of her belly with my index finger, leaving goosebumps in my wake. I shifted higher up her body and kissed her breast, leaving her nipple hard and waiting. She whimpered at my touch, making me smile.

Was it luck that we met or divine intervention? Regardless of the *how or why*, I was eternally grateful.

But there were thoughts swarming around in my mind that could drive us apart. There was no reason to doubt, but I did.

Why me?

I wasn't an alpha male who led the pack, nor was I rich. I was born human and created because of a bite from another were-leopard. I sought refuge with Léon, who had offered me a job securing his warehouse. And the Leap had taken me in as one of their own.

I stared down at Naomi, taking in each delicate feature. We might not travel the world, but I saw the stars glistening in her bright blue eyes.

There was something about Naomi I couldn't get

enough of, and thankful we had the rest of our lives to get to know each other. I would learn what made her scream while I made every inch of her body mine.

She was the one for me, and would protect and care for her with my life.

Our lives may not be perfect but I'd seen perfection under her clothes, and the loving and gentle way she touched me letting me know this was where I belonged. *With her.*

I was madly and deeply in love with her. If I died tonight, I'd gladly die in her arms.

"What's going on inside your head?" Naomi asked, pulling me out of my thoughts.

"If I had to die right now, this is where I'm supposed to be. Right here beside you."

Her eyes glistened like stars. She sat up, forcing me to sit too. She wrapped her arms around my neck and pulled me closer. I felt her heart beat against my chest.

Beast rushed to the surface.

My fangs emerged, desperately needing to make her ours. My mouth found the curve of her neck and I kissed her gently.

Naomi gasped and tilted her head back, giving me access to the vein in her neck. With hooded eyes and a nod, she pleaded. "Make me yours, Kai," she whispered. "I give you my heart, my body, and my soul. I am yours. Forever."

My fangs lengthened, and a low guttural sound came from the back of my throat. I wouldn't wait this time, nor did I feel her hesitation.

"You are mine, as I am yours." I claimed her as my one and forever, lowering my mouth against the side of her throat and my fangs pierced her delicate skin, filling my mouth with her sweet blood.

NAOMI

I barely felt the pinch of his bite against my neck as he claimed me. It was over so quickly, leaving behind a fierce need I had to fill.

Kai kissed up my jaw, each touch filled with emotion that spread through me like wildfire, making me light inside, as if floating on clouds. He gently caressed his lips against mine leaving me wanting more.

I craved his kisses and shifted closer. I wanted as much of my front touching as much of his, and knew this was where I belonged. *With him.*

A thrilling spark of desire moved through my body. The ache in my neck died down, leaving a hunger I never felt before.

I pulled back from Kai for a breath of air and met his dark gaze. His green eyes glowed as he raked them over my body, sending me over the edge with desire.

I traced my hands down the slabs of his chest, his taut nipples grazing my palms. Slowly, I worked my way down his body until I reached his hard shaft.

"Naomi," he said breathlessly, leaning back onto the bed and closed his eyes.

I wanted to give him what he desired and stroked downwards, revealing the crown. He pulsed against my hand. I licked up his shaft, and he shuddered beneath my touch. I covered him with my warm mouth, pulling a low growl from his lips. I was so engrossed with him; I didn't feel the bed move.

I squealed as he suddenly grabbed me and settled us in a seated position with me straddling his waist.

He claimed my lips with his, kissing harder, deeper, and needing more. I moaned as our bodies came into contact once more and his hard length pressed against my soft, delicate folds.

I wrapped my arms around his neck and clung to him as our tongues tangled; tasting copper. He lifted me and positioned himself, then slowly lowered me onto him, sending a wave of heat through my body. He angled his hips, filling me as he went deeper. I wanted to go fast, but savor every delicious inch of him.

Kai moaned when he reached the tip, and I gasped as he spread me wide. Our mouths claiming each other once more.

I lifted myself up then before he came all the way out, slowly sat down again. Kai held onto my hips to control my movement. I gripped his shoulders, digging my fingernails into his muscles, and arched forwards as I rode him.

I writhed, moving my hips in a circular motion with each careful thrust. I became a slave to my burning desire.

Kai moaned, his lips descended my body and stopped on a breast, tugging on a nipple as he drove deeper, harder and faster, finding his rhythm as it consumed me.

In that moment I gave myself over to Kai, riding him harder and faster. Kai responded by grunting and growling as he plunged into me on every downward thrust. It sent a cascade of thrills that only made me move faster as I sought release.

I lost myself in the actions. I didn't hear the primal sounds of our lovemaking. And I didn't comprehend our wild movements when I opened my eyes to watch Kai move from one breast to the other, he too lost in the moment.

The only thing I wanted was to be his.

I closed my eyes as we rocked against each other,

sealing our bond. Kai had bitten me, claiming what was his, while our lovemaking bonded us forever; heart, body, and soul.

He roared, deafening me. He jerked, his claws slicing the skin on my ass. I moaned, not remembering when his hands had shifted and wanted to scream in pleasure and pain as heat coursed through me at an alarming rate. Kai thrusted at the same time.

Pleasure and pain.

My blood heated as something started growing inside. It strengthened the powerful connection between us. The beginning of our bond, the beginning of our lives together, the beginning of our forever love.

Kai pumped into me, harder, and faster. I couldn't believe what I was doing, yet it felt natural; an extension of me, making me whole; a part of me I didn't know was missing—now complete. I felt intoxicated, addicted to him as our connection grew and flourished.

Our pleasure now bound. Our souls entwined. Our bodies one.

My heart thundered in time with Kai's. I felt his happiness in that glorious moment. I was safe; I was home.

Kai growled and roared again when I rocked my hips with his. He turned me onto my back as he continued his deep thrusting. He pulled my arms off his shoulders, linked our fingers above my head, palm to palm as our fingers clenched together.

Kai didn't hold back. Each wild and powerful movement tore a cry from me, unable to do anything but cling to him as he brought us over that pleasurable wave, sealing our fate.

Kai clutched me in place as he spilled inside. His eyes glowed as his body tensed and stilled. I squeezed around him as my orgasm exploded, and cried out as his name as I quivered.

The tension in my limbs melted away.

I licked my lips, my throat dry.

"Naomi?" he asked quietly, his voice filled with disbelief. He pressed a gentle kiss to my temple and slipped out, falling beside me on the bed.

I turned onto my side and smiled lazily. "I know," — I licked my lips again, — "That was… something else."

Chapter Thirty

NAOMI

When we arrived at the leap, Kai introduced me to leopards he was close to. Lee found a spot for us to sit on the grass waiting for the feast to begin.

Some leopards were getting the bonfire started. Others took care of the newer leopards, while some had already shifted and led down to the cages in the basement to eat and sleep.

I saw the man I met last week when Kai was shot and guessed he was the one who caught me when I fainted.

"Is that Sebastian?"

"Yes, with Blaire and their son, Zenon."

I squinted at the other man, who looked the same age as Sebastian. "The other guy looks as old as us. How can he be their son?"

"You know I told you Sebastian is half-vampire, half-leopard?" I nodded. "His and Léon's father, Salvador, turned into a vampire when he turned twenty-eight. From what Sebastian has told us both he and his brother aged quickly and have remained twenty-eight, like their father.

And since Zenon is Sebastian's, he too seemed to have aged rather quickly and stopped aging at the same age."

"She looks like she gave birth recently." I didn't mean for it to come out like that, but Blaire still had a little tummy and her hips curvy. I could tell she worked out, but she was still soft in places.

"Yeah, it's freaky crazy. Zenon was only born about four months ago."

"What?" My jaw slackened as I stared at the family. "Holy crap. And how old is Blaire?"

Kai turned to Lee, who shrugged. "I think she's in her forties."

"Shut the front door. She does not look forty." I closed my dry mouth, still not believing what I was seeing. "It's amazing, don't you think."

"There's Sacha." Lee pointed behind us.

Sacha and Michail walked with Greg, he was giving them the grand tour.

I met Greg when we arrived; he was the other leader of the Leap and shared the title with Sebastian. He was soft-spoken yet firm.

"I'm glad they're here, and I'm happy for my dad." I beamed at him and waved. When he saw us he waved back. I wondered whether Sacha would join the Leap permanently, but that was a question for another time; baby steps —he just resigned to the fact that I bonded with a leopard and would no longer be working for him.

"Yeah, I'm happy for him, too," Kai said.

I glanced around watching the others change form. I stared at my human hands that would stay human. I hoped my new family would accept me, as a human.

"I will always love you and the Leap has already accepted you," Kai said, pulling me closer.

"What? You read my thoughts?"

He grinned and kissed the top of my head. "Yes, babe, I sense your thoughts. I can't hear every word, but I know enough to answer your concerns. And you'll be fine while Lee and I hunt. There are others who have mated and are human and will remain near the bonfire. You can wait with them. Maybe make a friend or two."

Tears welled in my eyes as I stared at Kai's glowing green ones. I might not change into one, but my soul would be with him, running beside his leopard.

I moved closer, he purred when I pressed my hand against his chest, and kissed him in a forever kiss.

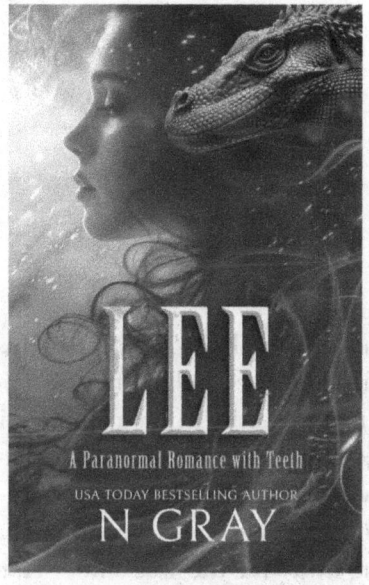

LEE

A Paranormal Romance with Teeth

USA TODAY BESTSELLING AUTHOR

N GRAY

www.vinci-books.com/lee

One night can change your everything.

When she stole my seat at the bar, I should've walked away. Instead, my wolf and I got tangled in her quest for an ancient egg thrumming with power. Now we're racing through dark streets, and I can't tell if it's magic or her touch making my skin burn.

Turn the page for a free preview…

Lee: Chapter One

I narrowed my eyes at Kai. He draped his arm lovingly around Naomi's shoulders, pulling her closer, and kissed her temple. I groaned inwardly at their public display of affection or my lack thereof. If they weren't such a cute couple, I would've slapped Kai just for the fun of it.

"Sorry, brother, I know it's your birthday, but Naomi and I are going away for the weekend," Kai said, wiggling his eyebrows.

"But why Camping? Of all the various activities, you go and decide to camp." I grumbled, not impressed. "You have a forest as a backyard," — the forest was near the warehouse, — "we hunt in the forest when the moon is full and now you want to camp in a forest…" I felt the lines between my eyes deepen.

When Kai kissed Naomi instead of responding, I continued speaking, "Where are you going and can I come with?" I grinned when Kai abruptly stopped showering his wife with love to show how disgusted he was with my comment.

"No, dude, it's our anniversary weekend away," Kai said, pushing against my shoulder. "And we aren't into threesomes." He held Naomi tighter as she giggled at our bantering. "But thanks for the offer anyway. If I'm ever desperate enough to make extra cash, I'll pimp your ass out to the bears. I hear they prefer smaller guys."

I couldn't help but laugh and admire my friend; he was one of a kind. "Good luck getting money out of anyone. Besides, you know I'll do it for free," I said, wiggling my eyebrows. We laughed at my terrible response.

Once I sobered, I added, "I get it, I really do. Enjoy your weekend lovebirds." I brought Naomi in for a hug and fist bumped Kai at the same time. "How long are you going away for? And does the boss know?" I glanced over my shoulder at the warehouse we called home.

"Yeah, I told Léon. He says it's fine." He slapped Naomi's ass when she walked away, sashaying. "I gotta go, brother," he said, grinning and wiggling his eyebrows.

"Don't worry," Flynn said, draping his arm around my shoulders. I narrowed my eyes at the were-lion; I should've heard him sneak up on me yet somehow I didn't. "I'll look after this one," Flynn added. "We all know he can't function like a man without his bestie."

I punched him in his stomach.

"Oof, easy there, leopard," he said, feigning injury.

"Back off, lion," I growled, pushing him away from me.

Flynn grinned, knowing he had succeeded in irritating me. It was one thing working with other shifters, but a different situation living with them, too.

Kai and I shared the same security shifts at the warehouse with two other shifters; Flynn, a were-lion, and Jude, a were-tiger. The four of us got on just fine but every now and then, like today, either Flynn or Jude irritated the crap out of me.

Léon, the Master Vampire of Sterling Meadow, had been around for centuries and had collected many items, some of which no one had been privy to seeing other than him. His priceless artifacts were kept at the warehouse we guarded because no insurance company could afford to insure the contents.

"Are we going out tonight?" Flynn asked enthusiastically.

I exhaled audibly and stared at him suspiciously. "Yeah, I suppose so. Why?"

"Okay, boys, I must go," Kai said, interrupting us. "See you in a couple of days." He waved over his shoulder as he walked toward his wife, who waited patiently for him at their vehicle, wearing a loving smile that would make any man's heart burst with pride.

"Don't you just hate those love-birds," Flynn added, heading back toward the warehouse. "Anyway, I'm going to check in with Jude and make sure he isn't breaking anything, then we can head out. I'm in desperate need of some tender flesh against my rock hard body."

"Me, too," I whispered.

"I hear you, buddy," Flynn called over his shoulder. "We're still waiting for our happily ever after." He stopped walking, turned around and glanced at me over his sunglasses, his yellow eyes blazing.

I tipped my head slightly in recognition. We were hard asses with our tough exterior, and like most shifters we needed to keep up with a certain facade, but deep down we all wanted to find our special someone. We all wanted the half of what we were missing to make us whole again.

Kai had just about given up when he met Naomi in the

club and they hit it off immediately, although they ran into some trouble with her father. But Kai had found his mate, and he couldn't be happier.

I sighed.

I needed to get my head out of the clouds and focus on securing the warehouse before heading out for drinks.

Lee: Chapter Two

It was my birthday, and I stood alone outside the bar like an idiot. Flynn had to rush back to the warehouse to help Jude with a huge delivery nobody warned us about. My usual wingman, Kai, was on a weekend away with his babe and I had… no-one.

I grunted my dissatisfaction regarding my predicament, glanced left and right, and groaned as groups of people headed my way. They laughed, some were drunk and tripped over their feet, while others spoke in hushed tones. They were human and just a group of friends enjoying their evening.

A jealously I hadn't felt in a long time struck with vengeance. Watching the group of friends made me realize how much I wanted a normal life filled with laughter and jealousy and evenings where I'd get drunk and sleep with an amazing woman who only wanted me more than any other man in the world.

But I knew I couldn't have any of that; my life was different. I was different. Everything about my job was different. I had to drink bottles of alcohol by myself before I felt the buzz and sleeping with a human female might hurt her if I wasn't careful. Everything I did had to be carefully thought about before I dared doing it.

I was stronger than most shifters and could kill a human male easily. Everything about my life as a supernatural in a human world was just that... different.

The group of laughing humans approached and the jealousy within me grew. Not wanting it to consume me, I had to get away from the humans and peered at the bar door, growling frustratingly. I didn't want to go back to the warehouse to stare at the television screen and I was tired of doing the same things daily. I needed a break and a change in scenery.

Instead of feeling sorry for myself I entered the local bar, warm air hitting me in the face before I had a chance to exhale. I hung my coat on the last empty hook near the door and scanned the venue for an open seat.

I headed toward the only available seat in a corner at the bar and, as I was about to sit, a curvy pint-sized woman stole the seat and called the barman to order a drink.

I growled.

Under normal circumstances I wouldn't behave aggressively toward a woman but she stole my seat on purpose. She knew I was about to sit down when she slid up beside me and took my seat. And the fact that she didn't bat an eyelash at her behavior only left me angry.

I growled again for effect.

The woman slowly glanced up, pushing her glasses up her nose to get a good look at me. Her dark blue eyes twinkled with humor as she brushed strands of hair that had fallen out of her bun off her shoulders. She turned away from me when the barman arrived and ordered a drink.

"You're in my seat?" I said, moving between her and the other patron, and leaned against the bar counter. I pushed my chest out so she could smell my aftershave; I practically bathed in the stuff.

She glanced at the floor, lifted her butt one cheek at a time, then turned to look up at me once more, narrowing her deep-blue colored eyes. "There's no name on the chair." She finished her retort with a wave of her hand, shooing me away.

I stared dumbstruck at this tiny, curvy thing with a big attitude and bunched my hands into fists, but I wouldn't hit her. I hit no one, let alone a woman, unnecessarily. I would hit back if a woman hit me first; just not as hard.

When the bartender returned he set her neat whiskey on the bar, I grabbed the glass and downed the contents.

"Hey!" she moaned, turning in the seat to look at me. "That was mine."

Once the honey liquid burned down my throat, I lifted the glass to see underneath. "There's no name, so I guess it could be anybody's." I shrugged nonchalantly, placing a note down; it was enough money to pay for the drink and a tip for the bartender. I then placed the glass on top of the money. "And don't steal the money, wench." I snapped my jaw at her as a warning.

She backed away from me with a tight smile on her face.

I pushed away from the counter and headed for my coat. Since there were no empty seats in the bar and after that altercation, I didn't feel like hanging around just to have her irritate me all evening. I thought drinking her beverage was enough punishment for stealing my chair and thought it best to get out of there while I had the last word.

As I traversed casually toward my coat I couldn't recall

from which direction she had come from, the curvy minx. I pulled on my coat and pushed the door open. Once outside, the cool air calmed me. I wiped my brow and pulled on my leather coat.

Flynn had dropped me off, but since he was no longer returning, I decided a brisk walk back to the warehouse would be better instead of calling him or a cab. It was a delightful evening for a stroll; the fresh air, stridulating insects, and a sky full of twinkling stars was what I needed to relax after that incident.

I sucked air over my teeth and caught the smell of fast-food and rain even though there were no clouds in the sky. The tension between my shoulder blades eased as I took in my surroundings in the quiet darkness, the noise of the bar long forgotten.

Being a were-leopard had its advantages; I had heightened senses, strength of fifty men, and eternal life; or until another supernatural being decided to end me. After my attack it was difficult for me to accept what I had been through and what I had become.

I'd go days not eating, not seeing friends, or leaving my room. All I wanted to do was die. I had thought my life was over. It took me a long time to realize my strengths but once I did, I used them to benefit me, and as motivation to live and move on with my life.

Not wanting to live eternity alone, I travelled the country trying to find others like me, and would accept me for who I was, and a place I could call home. Then one day I stumbled into Sterling Meadow, met Sebastian in the forest, and we clicked. Once he knew what I was and that I meant no harm, he invited me to join his leopards.

After a brief probationary period he introduced me to Léon, who offered me a job. It was pure luck that Kai and I joined the leopards at the same time, and we became friends soon thereafter.

After the attack, I was no longer allowed to prepare food for humans. And although I missed being a chef, I loved cooking for the guys at the warehouse. Every week I would try a culinary dish they had never heard of, ensuring my skills were on par even though I was never paid for it. I loved creating delectable dishes.

Deep in thought, I kicked a pebble and it skittered across the pavement and stopped at the next lamp post. The only thing I heard was my breathing and the surrounding insects.

I glanced up and saw the familiar warehouse in the distance, but before I headed in that direction, a car sped past. What happened next was quick: someone punched their hand through the window shattering it, sending shards of glass flew everywhere.

Something stung my cheek and when I wiped the area, my fingers came away with blood; but I healed quickly with little to no scarring.

The moment I saw a woman trying to climb out of the moving car, pushing her curvy body through the open window and screaming, I had to help.

Grab your copy...
www.vinci-books.com/lee

About the Author

A Multi-genre author writing twisted endings...

N Gray is a USA Today Bestselling Author who lives in Cape Town, South Africa, with her daughter and adopted cat named Miss Beans.

During the day, she's an analyst and provider profiler for a medical insurance company. At night, she types on her curved keyboard, creating fictional characters some may love and others you want to kill yourself.

She writes in four genres: urban fantasy, thriller, horror, and paranormal romance.

She now writes under Natalie Michaels for her new thrillers and SD Syns for her new horrors.

Acknowledgments

A special shout out to *Tammy at Book Nook Nuts* for helping me find the gremlins.

Thank you to my readers, old and new, for taking a chance on my books.

You are the reason I write the stories I do. As long as you keep reading, I'll keep writing.

I'm truly humbled by your support and encouragement.

I write in as many genres as I love reading in. There are so many stories swarming inside my head that I could never just choose one.

Horror is my guilty pleasure. I love writing short stories filled with dark humour and the occult with a twist ending.

Urban fantasy and paranormal romance are where I love to spend my time, and I have so many books planned that I don't have enough time (*but I'll get there*).

And lastly, my thrillers. Who doesn't love sitting on the edge of their seat while reading about what goes on inside the antagonist's mind? Well, I love writing about them.

www.ingramcontent.com/pod-product-compliance
Lightning Source LLC
Chambersburg PA
CBHW011750010726
47498CB00012B/3003